THE SHADES OF ELPHAME
GALLOWGLASS #1.5

JENNIFER ALLIS PROVOST

Copyright © 2024 by Jennifer Allis Provost

All rights reserved.

No portion of this book may be reproduced in any form without written permission from the publisher or author, except as permitted by U.S. copyright law.

Publisher's Note

This is a work of fiction. Names, characters, places, and incidents either are the product of the author's imagination or are used fictitiously, and any resemblance to actual persons, living or dead, business establishments, events, or locales is entirely coincidental. The scanning, uploading and distribution of this book via the Internet or via any other means without the permission of the publisher is illegal and punishable by law. Please purchase only authorized electronic editions, and do not participate in or encourage electronic piracy of copyrighted materials. Your support of the author's rights is appreciated.

Electronic Edition, License Notes

This ebook is licensed for your personal enjoyment only. This ebook may not be re-sold or given away to other people. If you would like to share this book with another person, please purchase an additional copy for each person. If you're reading this book and did not purchase it, or it was not purchased for your use only, then please purchase your own copy. Thank you for respecting the hard work of this author.

Cover by GetCovers

Contents

Author's Note	1
1. Weird Fairy Rocks	2
2. Bedeviled	9
3. The Unforgiven Dead	11
4. Survive	15
5. Forgiveness	20
6. Patience	24
7. Brightness	28
8. Possessed	31
9. Back to Elphame	35
10. Forthright	37
11. Cait Sith	41
12. Redcaps	45
13. Darkness	48
14. Caves	51
15. The Village Inn	55
16. Here	59
17. Thief	63
18. Refining the Ore	67
19. Master of Shadows	70
20. Know Better, Do Better	73

21. Life in the Sunlight	78
Also By Jennifer Allis Provost	80
About The Author	82

Author's Note

This novella is part of the Gallowglass urban fantasy series. It occurs about a week after the events in the first book. For more information on the series, including where to purchase, please see the information at the end of the story. Happy reading!

Weird Fairy Rocks

"I've got it," my brother, Chris, announced. "I'll call my next book *Les Ponts de Paris!*"

"The pants of Paris?" I asked. "That's... weird."

"Bridges of Paris," Chris corrected. "Pont means bridge."

"Then why don't you just call it *The Bridges of Paris*?" I asked. Chris and I were sitting at the kitchen table brainstorming ideas for his next book. That was proving to be no easy feat, since his last book, *Bones of the Bard*, had gone on to be a worldwide bestseller. He couldn't decide if he wanted to write about more dead Elizabethans, like he did in his last novel, or try something entirely new. I'd voted for new, and now we were talking about pants—I mean bridges—in Paris. "And would the book really be about bridges?"

"No. It would be about..." Chris leaned on the table and covered his face with his hands. "I don't know."

"Then let's start with the plot." A few days ago, I'd rescued my brother from the Seelie Queen's clutches. She'd been fascinated by his brilliant mind and tried to siphon off some of that brilliance for herself. This had the unfortunate effect of stifling Chris's creativity, and he became a sad, angry shadow of his former self. Now that he was free of her influence, the creative floodgates were open again, and much like a river after the spring thaw he was overflowing with ideas, though not all of them were top-notch. It was okay, though. Chris was back to his old self, and the good ideas would come. Eventually.

Along with Chris, I'd also rescued Robert Kirk from Elphame. He'd been kidnapped by the Seelie Queen centuries ago, and had spent most of the time since then serving as her gallowglass. That was a fancy name for a personal assassin. Now he was free of the queen, but he'd agreed to serve the Seelie King on occasion. Time would tell if that was a better, or worse, arrangement.

Actually, nothing could be worse than being enthralled by the Seelie Queen.

But now my brother the writer, and my boyfriend the assassin, were free, and all of us could move on with our lives. The first step was taking a trip home to New York, since I still had to finish my doctorate in geology, and Chris needed to return to his teaching job. I couldn't wait to resume our boring, fairy-less lives.

Robert had readily agreed to go to New York, though he'd thought I was kidding when I said we would fly there. Then I'd shown him the ticket booking website, and a few videos about planes and airports, and Robert declared he needed to take a walk. That had been two days ago, and Robert hadn't mentioned flights or planes since.

I hope he doesn't pass out when we get to the airport.

"About this plot," I said, since despite Chris's deepest desires this book wasn't going to write itself, "do you want to—hey!" Inexplicably, a handful of tiny stones landed on the kitchen table directly on top of my notebook. I held up one of the stones, and demanded, "Did you throw these at me?"

"Rina, of the two of us, who is more likely to have a pocketful of rocks?" Chris countered. "Are those from your collection?"

I poked at the uneven gray stones. "I don't collect gravel. Could they have fallen out of the ceiling?"

"Doubtful," Chris said, without looking up at me. "Who puts gravel in a ceiling? Fred Flintstone?"

"These rocks came from somewhere," I began, as I scanned the ceiling for gravel sized openings. I didn't see any holes or cracks. I was about to admit I was wrong when Robert strode in through the front door.

"Lunch has been acquired," he announced. There was a new panini restaurant next to the harbor, and Robert offered to scope the place out.

"What did you get us?" I asked, as he set the packages on the table next to Chris's notes. Even though they were both scholars—Chris had a doctorate in Shakespeare, of all things, and Robert held degrees in philosophy and divinity—they looked like complete opposites. My brother was tall, blond, and athletic, unlike short, brunette me. The only physical attribute we shared was our mother's blue eyes.

Robert's appearance was something else entirely. He was also tall, but instead of being merely athletic, these last few centuries he'd spent as Elphame's deadliest warrior had made him downright muscular. Add to that his dark, curly hair and pale blue eyes, and he cut quite the handsome figure, but Robert wasn't just an attractive man. He was also intelligent, and kind, and he was constantly doing little things to make me feel special. For instance, heading out to get our lunch.

"For Christopher and myself, there are two pressed sandwiches with ham and brie," Robert began, "and for you, my love, there is one made with cheese, tomato, and that mash of *pess toe* you so crave." He began opening the bag, then paused. "The table is filthy."

"Gravel rained down on us from out of nowhere," I said, as I swept the rocks into my hand. "Chris doesn't think it's a big deal."

"If you'd grown up with a sister that regularly hoarded piles of rocks, you'd be desensitized to random stones showing up on the kitchen table, too," Chris said, then he finally looked up from his work. "But I will admit that if they aren't Rina's, I have no idea where they came from."

"Thank you for humoring me." I set my handful of gravel on the windowsill, for lack of anyplace else to stash it, then I washed my hands. When I reached for the towel, Robert was beside me.

"Did the wee stones hurt you?" he asked.

"They landed on the table, not me." He nodded, and tilted his head as he scrutinized my arms for any wounds. Robert's concern made me concerned, mainly since I was hoping we'd have a long reprieve from all things Elphame.

"Do you think they could be magic stones?" I asked.

"Anything is possible, Karina love," Robert said. "However, if no one was injured, we can leave it for now."

"Great. I'm way too hungry to think about magic rocks."

Our paninis were, in a word, scrumptious. I didn't know what Robert's problem was with pesto, though. He needed to embrace more modern foods, and accept that people didn't live on mutton and bread any longer. Maybe I'll order us some salads for dinner, and try to convince him to eat more vegetables.

After we finished our lunch, Chris went into his room to do some work on his laptop, and Robert and I retreated to the couch. He was gradually warming up to the idea of watching television, though he only liked it in small doses. While I clicked around the channels, he alternated between frowning at the screen, and reading the newspaper he'd picked up in town. After cruising through every channel in the UK, I finally settled on one of the many versions of *Pride and Prejudice*.

"You'll probably like this," I said, as I set down the remote. "It takes place back when you were young, around two hundred years ago. Although, you were already past two hundred by then, weren't you?"

He narrowed his eyes at me over his newspaper. "Respect your elders," he said, but when he lowered the paper, I caught him smiling. "What's this about, then?" he asked, jerking his chin toward the television.

"There's five sisters, and they're all trying to get married." I fit myself in the crook of his arm. "But there's a big misunderstanding, and—ow!"

"Ow? Are you hurt?" Robert asked.

"Something hit my forehead." I rubbed the sore spot on my head, and looked down at my lap. There was another piece of gravel on my leg. "It's another tiny rock."

"Let me see that." Robert claimed the gravel, and examined it from every angle. "Seems to be a regular stone, but where did it come from?"

"Probably the same place as the rest, which is from up above." I went to the back closet where we kept the cleaning supplies, and dragged out the stepladder. "They've got to be falling out of the ceiling. There must be a crack, or something." I put the stepladder next to the couch and climbed upward.

"Karina love."

"What?" I swiveled around from the top of the stepladder so I could see Robert. He was standing in the center of the common room with his head tilted back as he turned in a slow circle.

"There are no cracks in the ceiling," he said. "And every bit of it is white plaster. Were the wee stones not a gray color?"

I looked up, and realized he was right. The ceiling was a flat, unmarred expanse of pristine white. There was no way these stones had come from the cottage's ceiling. "Could they have come through the window?"

"I suppose that is a possibility." He strode to the stepladder, then he grasped my hips and set me down on the floor. "However, I think the more likely explanation is what you said earlier."

"Magic stones?" I asked, and he nodded. "I was being sarcastic when I suggested that."

"Sarcasm or no, you may be on to something." Robert pushed my hair back from my forehead and examined the area.

"Is there a mark?"

"Aye, a small red spot where it got you. Does it hurt?"

"Not really."

Robert kissed my forehead, then he gathered me against him. "You're certain you're not hurt?"

"I am." I let myself enjoy being in his arms for a moment, resting against his warm, solid chest. Then my gaze landed on Chris's door.

"I hope Chris doesn't freak out about this," I said. "He's just starting to heal from everything Nicnevin did to him. I don't know how he'll react to weird stones flying out of thin air."

"He already saw the stones," Robert pointed out.

"I know. But he also decided they were somehow mine, and..." I leaned back, and met Robert's eyes. "I don't want to lie to him. I just don't want to tell him anything unless we're certain."

"I understand," Robert said, as he smoothed back my hair. "You've a tender, sweet heart, and you're willing to put it between your brother and anything that might hurt him."

"I am. And he'd do it for me."

"I have no doubt. Very well, my love, we'll keep this between us, and only involve Christopher if necessary."

I tightened my arms around Robert, and pressed my cheek against his chest. The second to last thing I needed was a weird fairy hanging around the cottage that liked to throw rocks. The absolute last thing was for those weird fairy rocks to hurt Chris.

Robert and I spent the rest of the afternoon watching Mr. Darcy pine over Lizzie Bennett, and dodging tiny stones as they flew around the cottage. The stones weren't threatening so much as annoying, but man did they sting when they made contact.

Although, the stones only ever struck me. By the time the movie was over, I'd been hit at least a dozen times, but Robert hadn't been hit once. When I shared my observation with Robert, he agreed that was odd.

"'Tis as if the stones are targeting you for some reason," he said. "Perhaps on account of your studies?"

"I have never heard a single story about a geologist getting attacked by stones," I said. "Believe me, I would remember that."

"I'm sure. I also have an idea."

"Lay it on me."

Robert's brow quirked. I would never admit it, but I greatly enjoyed his confused reactions to unfamiliar modern slang. "Why don't we leave the cottage, and see if the stones follow us?" he asked.

"Then we would know if it's a cottage problem or an us problem," I concluded. "I agree. We should take a walk into the village. Can you ask Chris if he wants to get out for a bit?"

"I thought we were shielding him from the stones."

"We can use this walk as an experiment, and update him afterward," I said. "Either way, once we have more information, it will be easier to make a plan."

"Very well," Robert said. "An experiment it is."

"Awesome. I'm going to change."

While Robert told Chris we were heading into the village, I went to the bedroom to swap out my sweatpants for jeans. After I'd shed the sweatpants, I caught a glimpse of my reflection, and gasped. My legs were covered with tiny bruises. I leaned closer to the mirror and pushed up my hair. Just like Robert had said, there was a black and blue mark near my hairline. The fact that the bruises had darkened so quickly was a telltale indicator of magic.

Great. Since I couldn't do anything about the bruises at the moment, I pulled on my jeans and grabbed my boots, and rejoined Robert in the common room. Hopefully, all of these bruises would heal before Robert got a look at them. As a rule, gallowglasses had pretty short fuses, and nothing made Robert angrier than when he thought I'd been hurt.

Bedeviled

Chris was down for a walk, and soon enough, the three of us were heading toward the center of the village. It was almost autumn, but the weather was still warm and the sun was bright and glorious. As much as I was homesick for my apartment in Queens, I was going to miss living in this little fishing village.

We were approaching the old toll booth when I felt the first ping. It was sharp, and had hit the back of my arm just beneath the edge of my sleeve. Not wanting to worry the other two, I ignored it, just like I ignored the next few strikes. Then a stone hit the side of my neck—hard—and I gasped.

"What is it?" Robert demanded. "More stones?"

"Yeah." I showed him the side of my neck. "I've been hit at least five times."

Robert glowered at me. "Only five?"

"Hit?" Chris asked. "Hit by what?"

"Whatever is causing these wee stones to fly about, they're fixating on Karina," Robert said. My stomach turned when he said that, but he was right. For whatever reason, these stones were after me.

"Why are they only hitting Karina?" Chris demanded.

"We do no' ken," Robert replied, then he turned to me. "Where else are you hurt?"

"All over, really." I looked up at Robert. "What would do this?"

Before Robert could reply, a stone the size of my fist hurtled through the air and struck my ankle. I cried out and dropped to the ground, as another stone flew into my back and slammed into my kidney. The pain shocked me, and I went down on my side.

"Enough," Robert bellowed. He'd summoned his sword and shield from the magical place they hung out in when he didn't need them. Now he stood over me, scowling at the air. "Show yourself!"

A rock flew through the air. Robert whacked it aside with his sword as Chris crouched beside me.

"Get out of the line of fire," I said. My vision blurred, and I felt hot tears on my face. "I don't want you getting hit!"

"I'm trying to protect you," Chris snapped, only to be drowned out by the sound of metal reverberating as Robert blocked another rock with his shield. "What's happening?"

"I really don't know," I said, then I spied movement across the street. In the shadows cast by a stand of trees was something that looked like a bundle of rags. The bundle twitched, and more rocks struck Robert's shield. I pointed toward the shadows, and yelled, "Robert, there!"

Robert's gaze followed my outstretched arm, then he picked up the rock that struck my back and threw it toward the creature. The rock made contact with the creature, then it shrieked and fell forward. Finally, it disappeared in a puff of smoke.

"Did you see that?" I asked Chris.

"Yeah. There were rag monsters like that at Nicnevin's place." Chris frowned, and added, "They didn't throw rocks, though."

"T'was no rag monster," Robert said. "Karina, you're bedeviled by one of the sluagh."

The Unforgiven Dead

Since my ankle was all but useless, Robert carried me home. Being in his arms made me feel safe, as if whatever monsters were after me didn't stand a chance against the gallowglass. Chris, however, wasn't taking any chances. He carried Robert's shield, his gaze tracking back and forth as he watched for projectiles. But nothing was thrown at us, and the walk home was short and uneventful.

Once we were inside the cottage, Robert laid me on the couch, then he removed the shoe and sock from my injured ankle. I shivered as the cool air hit my bare, swollen skin.

"Can you move your foot?" he asked.

I wiggled my toes. "Yeah. Hurts, though." I twitched my ankle, and grimaced as pain shot up my leg. "I think I'll be hopping for a while."

"What the hell is a sluagh?" Chris demanded.

"They're the unforgiven dead, doomed to walk the earth for eternity," Robert replied. "Unless the devil captures them, and brings them to hell, or the Wild Hunt rounds them up and transports them to Elphame."

"Why is that monster after Rina?" Chris demanded, as he flung open the freezer door. "And why don't we have any ice?"

"Just wet down a towel," I said to my brother, then I faced Robert. "Do you think Nicnevin sent it after me?" I asked, even though mentioning the Seelie Queen by name wasn't smart. The pain made me want answers as soon as possible.

"T'would be a bit heavy-handed for her," Robert replied. "In all the years I served her she dealt with her enemies in one of two ways. She would either slowly drive them mad, or have them killed swiftly and painfully. Tossing stones at you doesn't accomplish either."

"Then why is this creature after Rina?" Chris sat on the far end of the couch and lifted my ankle onto his lap, then he wrapped the cool, wet towel around it. That sent shivers up my entire body, so I grabbed the throw blanket and snuggled in. "That should help with the swelling. Do we have any ibuprofen?"

"If we do, it's in the medicine cabinet," I replied. Chris went to the bathroom in search of anti inflammatories. Robert claimed the spot Chris had vacated, and eased my foot onto his lap.

"You think it was a sluagh?" I asked. I knew next to nothing about those creatures, other than they hated me.

"Aye. They are tricksters, and known to keep to the shadows and cause problems for the living."

"Oh. Great." I tried moving my ankle again. That was a bad idea. "Is it trying to kill me?"

"I've never heard of one behaving in such a manner. I've seen them harry mortals before, but it damn near crushed your ankle."

"The way the stones hit me," I began, remembering the little explosions of pain. "It was almost like the sluagh was angry. But why would one of those creatures be mad at me?"

"I don't know, Karina love, but I swear to you I will find out."

After Chris brought me two ibuprofen and a glass of water, he filled the ice trays and set them in the freezer. When the freezer wasn't making ice fast enough, he declared he would go into town and purchase a bag of ice. As soon as he was out the door, Robert picked me up and brought me into our bedroom.

"What's this all about?" I asked, as he set me on the bed.

"I need to know where else this beast has hurt you," he said. "Will you show me?"

"Yeah. Give me a hand." I unbuttoned my jeans, then Robert helped me pull them off my already swollen ankle; at this rate, it was going to end up the size of a watermelon. Robert frowned when he got a look at my black and blue speckled legs.

"That looks painful," he said.

"It is. There's some on my back, too." I sat up and pulled off my shirt, and turned so Robert could see my back; the stones had peppered the area between my shoulder blades, and I knew it must look awful. He was deathly quiet for a moment, then he sat beside me and touched the bottom edge of my tank top.

"One got you lower down, did it not?"

I nodded, and he eased that last layer up and over my head. His fingers grazed my lower back, and I flinched when he brushed against a sore spot.

"Forgive me, Karina love," he murmured. "I... I do not know how to help you. I have never afore encountered something like this, and I can't help but feel as if this is my fault."

"How could any of this be your fault?" I asked, wincing as I turned to face him. "Tell me what you know about the sluagh. Please."

"When the Wild Hunt rides, we attempt to round them up, but a few always slip through our fingers. Catching one is akin to grasping a shadow."

"Did you ride in a lot of these Wild Hunts?"

"I did," he replied, only to frown when I shivered. "Here, get under the blankets."

"Stay with me?" I asked. "I'm so cold."

Robert stripped off his shirt and put his warm body against my cold one, and I my frigid muscles begin to thaw. "Does the sluagh make people cold, too? I feel like I was outside naked in winter."

"They congregate in the shadows, so I imagine they're naturally colder than we are." One of his hands cupped the back of my head, while the other slid down to my bottom. Just like that, I went from barely warm to nearly overheated. "When the Hunt goes forth, we find the sluagh by following the icy winds left in their wake."

"Did you like riding with the Hunt?" My nose was pressed against Robert's neck. He smelled so good, musky and warm, but with an undertone of the lavender soap we used.

"I did," he murmured, with his lips against my forehead. "It was one of the few times whilst in Elphame I felt free." He laughed shortly. "It was one of the few times I felt like a man."

"How could you ever not feel like a man?" I trailed my fingers down his chest to his abdomen, and hooked them in his belt. "You've got to be the most masculine person I've ever met."

"Aye?" Robert moved so I was underneath him, and nuzzled my neck. "I feel rather masculine now."

I unfastened his pants and took his hot, heavy cock in my hand. "Yeah? Want to do something about it?"

He kissed me breathless. Somehow he got the rest of our clothes off of us without breaking the kiss, then he was thrusting inside me. Sex with Robert was amazing in a way I never thought it could be; before the first time we'd been together, I'd thought those movies scenes of women screaming and convulsing in pleasure were nothing but fiction.

Now I grabbed onto his shoulders as he drove himself into me, deeper and deeper until I felt the edge of my orgasm creeping up. Robert drew back so he could see my face; he liked to watch me come. I met his gaze, and screamed.

Instead of Robert, the sluagh was staring down at me.

Survive

"What's wrong?" I demanded. In the midst of me loving her, Karina had screamed bloody murder. "Are you hurt?"

"The monster," she began, as she pushed me off her and retreated to the farthest corner of the room. "I looked up, but the sluagh was there instead of you!"

"What?" I glanced in the mirror, but my face was my own. "How is that possible?"

"I have no fricken' clue." She picked up her discarded shirt, and held it in front of her breast. I moved toward her, but she cowered away from me. "I-I think I need a minute alone."

"Very well." I collected my clothing, and withdrew to dress in the bathroom.

Now I sat at the kitchen table, alone as I should be. The sound of Karina's scream still rang in my ears, and the image of her terrified face greeted me every time I closed my eyes. Somehow, some way, the sluagh had put itself between her and I at our most intimate moment, and I didn't know how to keep that from ever happening again.

I also didn't know if Karina would ever look at me the same way ever again, much less make love to me. The way she'd shrieked, and pushed me away as she scrambled out of our bed...

The bedroom door opened. I turned, and saw Karina limp into the common room. She was wearing the fuzzy pink robe she favored, and I could see the bruises on her legs and neck, her red and swollen ankle, and that awful mark on her forehead. Good lord, she looked like she'd been on the losing side of a battle.

"Karina," I began.

"I didn't mean to yell at you like that." She crossed her arms over her stomach. "When I saw that face, it was..." She swallowed, and looked out the window toward the garden. "It was terrifying."

"I am so sorry, love," I began, but she shook her head.

"It wasn't your fault. Where... where do you think it went?"

"They gravitate toward darkness, and shadows."

"Great, so it's in my closet?" she demanded, her voice going shrill with fear.

"Karina. Love." When she wouldn't look at me, I stood and approached her. It nearly killed me to not touch her, but it was plain that physical contact was the last thing she needed. "I swear to you, I will find this creature, and I will end it. It will torment you no more."

"And then what?" she asked. "Will some other monster ooze out of Elphame and into our life? Will some other wee beastie throw rocks at me until I'm in so much pain I can barely move?"

She sobbed at the last, and despite everything, I took her into my arms. "Don't cry," I crooned. "I have you. I'll keep you safe, from the sluagh and every other creature on earth and in Elphame." When she only sobbed harder, I asked, "Do you believe me? Karina, love, please talk to me... Or if you don't want to talk, I understand. I'll leave you be, and wait until you're ready."

"Don't go," she said. "I believe in you."

Christopher reentered the cottage, his arms laden with bags from the chemist's shop. "I got painkillers, ice packs, some bandages," he began, then he spied the two of us holding each other. "What happened?"

"Nothing," Karina said, as she slid out of my arms. She affected a smile that did not reach her eyes, and nodded toward the bags. "Did you buy out a hospital?"

"It doesn't look like nothing," Christopher pressed. "You're both upset and you're covered in bruises. Did the creature come back?"

"I don't want to talk about it," she snapped.

"Well I do want to talk about it," Christopher said, then he faced me. "What the hell did you let happen to her?"

"I did not *let* anything happen," I all but growled. "I defend Karina with my body and blade!"

"Looks like you're doing a shit job," Christopher said.

"Chris, leave it," Karina said.

"No," Christopher snapped. "How are all these rocks getting past you, the supposedly legendary warrior?"

I took a step toward Christopher, my fist clenched. "Do not test me," I snarled. "I've lived amongst these monsters since before your grandparents drew breath. I can protect Karina from the sluagh, of that you can be sure."

"Then why is she crying?" Christopher yelled.

"Robert and I were fucking and the sluagh got between us," Karina shrieked. "There, is that what you wanted to know? Are you satisfied? Now both of you, leave me alone."

Karina didn't wait to see our reactions. Instead, she limped back to the bedroom and slammed the door.

I spent the next hour or so in the back garden, practicing my swordplay. For all that I'd wanted to spend my life as a scholar and nothing more, it was engaging in physical activity that allowed my mind to roam free. Before I'd gone underhill, I performed chores around the farm, my muscles heaving and back sweating as I tended to the livestock or other tasks, while my mind worked out problems or composed prose. Now I swung and parried my sword as I contemplated exactly how I would kill the sluagh.

And the sluagh was going to die. For how it had terrified my dearest Karina, I would make sure its death was slow and painful.

After a time, Christopher entered the garden. He sat on the stone bench near the roses, and the wights alighted on his arms and shoulders. Even their colorful wings didn't cheer him.

"Are we good?" Christopher asked.

"Of course," I replied, as I lowered my sword. We'd only shouted at each other out of our mutual concern for Karina. "How is she?"

"Better, at least physically. She let me wrap up her ankle, and she took some painkillers. Rina's tough. She'll be okay."

"She shouldn't have to be tough, or okay." I sat beside Christopher and leaned back, my gaze on the clouds rushing by overhead. "Karina shouldn't have to deal with any of this. She deserves more than being with someone like me. Thanks to my past, these creatures will always seek us out."

"I think you're being a little hard on yourself."

"Am I? The whole time I've been out here, I've plotted how to murder the sluagh. Not just the one from earlier, but all of them. Death is how I solve all my problems, ever since that first time Nicnevin pitted me against her assassin." My victory over than man is what led to me becoming the gallowglass. I'd had many challengers since then, and defeated every one.

And now I was being outsmarted by a shade.

"But you survived that first assassin, and I think that's the key," Christopher said. "After our parents died, I became Rina's legal guardian. It was an unusual situation, but it worked for us, and everything was fine for a few years. Then, when Rina was around fifteen, sixteen, she transformed from a cute kid into a beautiful young woman, and I was terrified."

"Because you worried you wouldn't be able to protect her?" I asked.

"That, and because Rina did not want me getting between her and her problems. She wanted to be able to protect herself," he replied. "So I signed us up for some self-defense classes. When we went to the first lesson, the instructor told us that the first rule of self-defense isn't to kill or incapacitate your enemy. It's to survive."

"Survive," I repeated.

"Exactly. You don't need to be the biggest or strongest or meanest. You just need to get past whatever's in your way, and keep going. Just like how you got past everything you dealt with in Elphame, and how I got past Rina growing up and not needing me anymore. We just need to get to the other side."

"The other side. Christopher, you're brilliant."

"Care to share whatever epiphany I've helped you reach?"

"I am going to round up the sluagh and send them back to the other side."

Forgiveness

I went inside the cottage, and found Karina near comatose from the pills Christopher had given her.

"Why is Karina so drowsy?" I asked Christopher. "A mere hour ago, she was wide awake and lucid."

"It's a side effect of the painkillers," he replied. "They always knock her out for a while. Don't worry, she's okay."

While I trusted Christopher, I did not care for his explanation. In my day, if you administered a wort to a body and they became a near incoherent shadow of their former vibrant, intelligent, compassionate self, you'd be accused of witchcraft. Then again, we weren't in my day, and I kent well those people hadn't been witches, just poor crofters attempting to make sense of a confusing world.

"You're certain?" I pressed. "She will wake from this?"

"I am," Christopher replied. "They're reducing her pain, and the inflammation from the bruises. The medication is helping her heal."

I nodded, then I sat beside Karina and smoothed back her hair. Her forehead was damp, but she didn't appear feverish. Most likely she was warm thanks to the multitude of blankets piled on her.

"Karina love," I began, "I'm going to collect the sluagh and send them back where they came from. They shall harm you no more."

"Okay," she mumbled into her pillow. "I'll just take a little nap while you guys hang out."

I kissed her cheek. "Rest for me, mo chroí. I shall return anon."

"Anon," she said, then she slipped into sleep. I stood, summoned my armor, and left in search of the sluagh.

I'd had much experience with the sluagh, and near all of it was from my time spent leading the Wild Hunt. Every winter, Nicnevin and Fionnlagh had ridden forth on matching white steeds, myself directly behind the queen on my own dun horse, and as we crossed the heavens from Elphame and into the mortal world, we collected what souls we could. The sluagh had always been the most challenging to catch, and only partly due to their ethereal form. Most assumed that we were sent by the devil himself to bring them to hell, and they were terrified of us.

Now that I thought about it, the sluagh were the only creatures who had felt such abject fear of the Hunt. As I considered that, I recalled the many joyous rides I'd taken part in. When I told Karina how much I'd enjoyed riding in the Hunt, I'd meant it. Every member of the Seelie Court looked forward to the Hunt, and competed for positions close to the king and queen. And I had been right there beside Nicnevin, duty-bound as always, and watched her grinning like a fool as she rounded up the sluagh like wildflowers in a meadow.

At first, I wondered if these attacks on Karina were an act of revenge by the sluagh against me, but I dismissed that thought rather quickly. The sluagh were the unforgiven dead, and were damned to walk the mortal plan for eternity. They had no natural association with one another that remained from their time among the living. A sluagh would no more take revenge against me for capturing one of its kind than I would hold a grudge against bears because one had eaten a person long ago. But if revenge wasn't their motivation, what was?

The sun dipped low, casting long shadows across the village. That was good, since shadows were where I worked best. Some of Elphame's warriors craved glory, and made a show of every bout they faced so all would know their names, but not me. Whenever I was given a mission, I slipped through the shadows until I found my prey, and silently slit their throat. In time, the shadows of Elphame became a comfort to me, and the dark, welcoming shade of the mortal world functioned in much the same way.

Perhaps my fate was to become one with the sluagh. If I died today, would I be forgiven? Would my soul be doomed to wander the earth, alone for eternity? Would God look kindly upon me, or have the fell deeds I committed at Nicnevin's behest erased any and all good I've done?

I shook my head. It wasn't the time or place for such thoughts. There would be plenty of time to consider my immortal soul's fate once the sluagh were gone, and Karina was safe. I stopped walking, and took stock of my surroundings. In front of me was the ancient parish kirk. On occasion, I longed for the simpler days when I was the minister of my small kirk in Aberfoyle, before I'd lost my first wife and plunged myself into research about the Good People. But now I had my Karina, my dear one, and even though it had taken me several lifetimes to find her, I was convinced that she and I were meant to be together.

As I gazed at the kirk, I imagined Karina and I attending services, sitting in rapt attention as we listened to the minister's sermon. Neither she nor her brother were ones for attending mass, and truth be told, I hadn't seen the inside of a kirk in a very, very long time. Just as I resolved to ask Karina if she would like to accompany me to next Sunday's mass, I spied movement in the shadows on the far side of the kirkyard.

Sluagh.

I strode across the yard, sword out. It wasn't like me to be so brazen, but these creatures had harmed Karina, and there was no way I was letting them out of my sight. As for the sluagh, it made no attempt to conceal itself, or escape.

"Why have you seen fit to harass my Karina?" I demanded.

"Why have you left us?" the shadow beast countered. "Why do you not care for us any longer?"

"I never cared for you one way or the other," I said. The first sluagh was joined by two others, and they swirled around my body like smoke rings. "I only ever saw your kind during the Wild Hunt."

"Yes, and you brought those that came before us to Elphame," the three said as one. "You sent them on to a new life. You were our only hope. Now we are trapped, and are doomed to walk in darkness until the end of time."

"But why harry Karina?" I demanded. "She has nothing to do with your fate."

"She is the reason you left us," they hissed. "Without her, you will return to Elphame. Without her, you will help more of us."

"That's where you're wrong. I will never return to Elphame, not if I can help it." The creatures wailed, and I raised my sword with grim determination. It served them right to be damned, and it served them right to be miserable. How dare those who were already damned seek help from me? Me, a man of God?

I paused, my sword heavier than usual in my hands. Was I not just concerned for my own soul's fate? Was I not concerned that God would judge me harshly, and damn me to a similar fate to the sluagh? Or perhaps He would not judge me harshly. Perhaps damnation is the fate I've earned.

Perhaps the sluagh had been judged harshly. I did not know a single thing about these creatures, not how they'd lived their lives or how they had died. When I'd been a minister, my purpose had been to help people, regardless of who they were or what they'd done.

The sluagh were no different. I had no notion of how these souls had ended up as unforgiven dead, but it wasn't for me to judge them. What they needed was help, and that was something I could do.

"Is that what you really want?" I asked. "Not to hurt Karina, but to move on?"

"Yes," they wailed. "Yes, yes. We must ascend to the next plane, but we do not know how."

I turned toward the kirk, and nodded. "I may ken a way to help you, but first you must swear to me that you will never again harm Karina. No rocks, no appearing in front of her, nothing. Karina means more to me than anything in this or any world, and she is to be protected at all costs."

"We agree," they said, their voices layered like a choir. "We shall keep Karina safe."

"Very well," I said. "Wait here."

Patience

I was on track to have the worst day in history. I'd been pelted by rocks, attacked by shadow monsters, and to top it off, I'd yelled at Robert. My brother—who had remained carefully neutral after my outburst about the sluagh sneaking into my and Robert's bed—had given me a few pain pills, and I went back to bed with the hope that this was all a very bad dream.

Some time later, I sat bolt upright in bed. I had no idea how long I'd been asleep, or if gravel was still flying around the cottage. Then I remembered Robert coming to see me, and telling me that he was going out to round up the sluagh.

What did that mean? And where the hell had Robert gone?

I got myself dressed, and hobbled out to the common room. Chris was sitting on the couch, reading a book. He set it aside when he saw me.

"Hey, how are you feeling?" he asked. "Want anything to eat?"

"Where's Robert?" I demanded.

"He went after the sluagh," Chris replied. "You don't remember? You were pretty out of it when he told you."

I sat next to Chris. "He really went alone?"

"Rina, he's the best person for the job," Chris said, and that was the truth. Robert had spent hundreds of years among Elphame's monsters, and knew more about them than almost anyone. "He'll be fine."

"But we don't know how many sluagh there are," I said. "What if they gang up on him? What if they hurt him?"

"Rob seemed pretty confident," Chris said. "He's not going to kill them. He said he'll round them up and send them back to Elphame." I must have looked skeptical, because he added, "I think we can let him handle this."

"The last time I saw him, I yelled at him," I said. "What if I never get to apologize?"

"Rina, he understands why you were upset," Chris soothed. "He's not mad at you."

I nodded, because Chris was right. Robert did understand why I'd been so upset, which was why he took off and decided to rid the world of every stray sluagh on his own. My mouth went dry, either due to a side effect of the medication or my worry over Robert. "I just want him to come home."

"He will," Chris said. "We just need to be patient."

At first, I was patient. Then I was anxious, and angry, and by the time I'd waited four hours for Robert to come home, I was so desperate for his return I drew up an entire plan for me to follow him into Elphame. Only, I didn't know if he'd gone to Elphame, or some other alternate dimension, or if he was still right here in Crail having a beer at the local pub; okay, maybe not that last one. Still, there was nothing I could do to help Robert, and that just sucked.

Eventually, I fell asleep on the couch. I was woken by a warm, calloused hand on my cheek. I blinked my eyes open, and saw Robert standing over me. He didn't look like he'd been fighting for his life against untold monsters. In fact, he was smiling at me.

"You're here," I said, as I sat up and threw my arms around his neck. "I'm so sorry I yelled at you. It wasn't your fault!"

"No need to be sorry, my love," he said, as he slid his arms around me. "And no need to be afeared any longer. I've dealt with the sluagh, and they will never again harm you."

"How did you deal with them?" I drew back, but held onto his hands. "Did you summon the Wild Hunt?"

"I did not. Instead, I considered the nature of the sluagh. The unforgiven dead, they're called, and as I stood in the kirkyard it occurred to me. What would happen if I forgave them?"

I blinked. "You can do that?"

"Not exactly, for only God can truly forgive. However, I did hie myself into the kirk, where I requested a measure of holy water. I used the water to bless each and every sluagh I came across. They disappeared, but not before appearing at peace. I assume they have finally moved on, and they're now in a better place."

"That's amazing," I said. "Look at you, rescuing a bunch of angry dead people, even though they tossed boulders at my head."

His eyes widened. "Are you upset with me?"

"No, but..." I released his hands, and rubbed my eyes. "You're this badass warrior who can handle all these magical monsters, but you send the ones that left me a black and blue mess on to a better life?"

"I never wanted to be, as you put it, a bad ass warrior," he said quietly. "I may still be the Seelie King's gallowglass, but I no longer wish to solve all my problems with death and killing. I want to be a better man, and make myself worthy of you."

I'd never gone from anger to total, complete love in less than a minute, but Robert's words touched something deep within me. "You don't need to do anything to be worthy of me," I said. "You're you, and that's enough. It's more than enough." I set my hand on his cheek. "And I'm very proud of you, for finding a non-lethal way to deal with the sluagh."

Robert grinned, then he turned his head and kissed my palm. "Are you, now?"

I returned his smile. "I surely am."

"While I am glad to end their suffering, I was most concerned with rescuing you," he said. "Karina my love, I meant what I said. I will protect you from all beasts, be they from earth or Elphame, for as long as I am alive."

"I believe you." I moved to stand, but my sore ankle had other ideas. "Want to carry me back to bed?"

"I thought you'd never ask."

Brightness

The next morning, I woke to a cursed sunbeam streaming directly onto my face. I swore, then I reached out and snapped the curtain shut.

"What's wrong?" Karina asked. She rolled over and pressed herself alongside me, her cheek against my throat. "You always leave the curtains open in the morning."

"'Tis a bit bright out today," I replied, but she was right. After all the time I'd spent in the bowels of Nicnevin's castle, and then trapped within the Minister's Pine, I craved sunlight. Up until this morning, I'd thought the brighter the better, but now the sunlight seared my eyes and made my head throb in agony. I moved toward the curtains to pull them tighter, and shielded my eyes against the strip of light coming from underneath the drapery. "It doesn't seem brighter to you?"

"It's just regular sun."

"You didn't even look," I accused. She hadn't moved from her nest of blankets. Truth be told, I didn't want her to move, either.

"I looked earlier." She caressed my cheek, then drew back and scrutinized my face. "You, however, are colder than usual. Maybe you're sick."

"Bah," I said. "I haven't been sick in centuries. The elixir keeps me well and hale." The Seelie elixir was a blend of herbs and magic, and it helped one's form heal faster than normal. Karina had also sampled it on occasion, and I hoped it would heal her wounds from the day prior. "How are your bruises, and your ankle?"

"Much better," she replied, with a smile that warmed me as no fire ever could. "My ankle is hardly sore at all."

"Wonderful news," I said, as I smoothed back her hair. Karina meant everything to me, and to know she was recovering well eased my own guilt of having brought the sluagh on her in the first place. "How would you like to spend the day?"

"Hmm." She slid an arm and a leg across my body. I understood what was on her mind, but we couldn't spend the entire day in bed, again. Well, perhaps half a day would be all right. It wasn't as if I could ever get enough of her.

"Since we'll be going to New York soon, why don't you decide what we do today?" she suggested. "I mean, we can always come back, but it'll be a while before we're in Scotland again. Is there any place you'd like to see?"

Yet again, Karina's kind heart humbled me. "Why don't we take a walk along the coast," I suggested. "We can smell the good sea air, and feel the sand beneath our feet. Perhaps we'll come across a lovely spot for a bite, as well. We can begin by walking down to the village, to test if your ankle's up for more of the trail," I added.

"That's a great plan. We can get going in around an hour."

"An hour? Why an hour?"

She moved so her face was above mine, and she was wearing the most devious grin. "If you don't know, I'd better show you."

Two hours later, I realized what a horrible idea I'd had.

The vicious, overly bright sun beat down on the back of my neck and threatened to roast my skin like a joint of mutton. What's more, the light reflected off every surface imaginable, and my eyes ached from the glare. I had no idea if there was a god or fairy or a thrice bedamned demon behind the sun, but I had surely offended whatever controlled the fiery orb in the sky.

"Robert." Karina slid her palm against mine. "What's wrong?"

"'Tis bright out, nothing more," I said. Not only was the brightness the direct cause of my misery, I did not wish to worry Karina by sharing the true extent of my discomfort. We would be indoors soon enough, and my torment would end.

"You're sure it's just that?"

I wasn't, but I didn't want to share that. Not yet. "What else could it be?"

"Who knows, but I can help with the brightness." She dug around in her bag for a moment, and produced a pair of dark spectacles. "These sunglasses will dim things a bit."

I accepted the spectacles, and perched them on the bridge of my nose. With the addition of the glasses, everything was just as bright and my head throbbed just as much, but now the world was cast in a brown overtone. "Thank you, love."

"They're not helping, are they?" Before I could respond, Karina stood herself in front of me, then she stretched up on her toes and began feeling my forehead and neck. I ducked my head, and looked at her over the top of the spectacles. When she put her palm against my cheek, she gasped.

"What is it?" I asked.

"You're still cooler than normal," she replied in a rush. "We should go back to the cottage, and you should get back in bed."

"You didn't have enough time in bed with me earlier?" I asked. She blushed, but my reference to how I'd loved her wasn't enough to sway her from the notion that I was ill.

"Very funny. If anything, I wore you out." She wound her arm through mine, and tugged me back the way we came. "Come on, let's get you out of the sun so you can recover from whatever this is."

"As you say, love." I kissed the top of her head. "You take very good care of me."

"Don't you forget it."

Possessed

I did my best to smile and laugh as Robert and I walked back to the cottage, but inside I was screaming. When I stood in front of Robert so I could feel his forehead, the sunglasses had slipped down his nose. I reached up to straighten them, and saw his eyes. Instead of seeing myself reflected in his pale blue eyes, I saw a host of sluagh staring back at me.

Robert was possessed by the exact same creatures that had used me for target practice, and I had no idea what the extent of the sluagh's control was. Were his words his own, or the monsters'?

"Och," he said, as he raised his hand to shield his eyes from the sun. "This light is determined to set my very mind afire."

I glanced toward our left. In an effort to keep Robert away from any innocent bystanders, I'd taken the coastal path back to the cottage, instead of going through the village. This way was longer, but I'd assumed it would be safer for everyone. Now the glare off the ocean was irritating the sluagh trapped in his eyes even more than the sun was.

The only new aspect about this situation was that unlike the day before, the sluagh were only tormenting Robert. No rocks were flying through the air, and that was a definite improvement. Despite that, I couldn't let them make Robert suffer, and he was definitely suffering.

"Let's find some shade," I said, as I tugged him toward some sandstone caves. "I think getting out of direct light will do you some good."

"Aye," he mumbled. I got him inside the cave and helped him sit against the wall. Slightly more terrifying than the monsters in his eyes was the fact that I was guiding Robert around like a child, and that was just crazy. Whereas I was of below average height and build, Robert was over six feet tall and built like a linebacker. I shouldn't be able to lead him anywhere. What's more, he was the gallowglass, the legendary warrior feared across Elphame. Now, thanks to the sluagh who had taken up residence inside him, he was little more than a stumbling man.

But how had this happened so suddenly?

I crouched in front of him, but my sore ankle didn't like that. I ended up kneeling in the dirt, and took his hands. "Talk to me," I said. "You were fine at home. Now you're acting like you can barely navigate around. What happened?"

"The light," he replied. "I cannot explain it, but I feel as if the light is sapping my strength. The brighter it shines, the weaker I get."

"Show me your eyes."

Robert removed the sunglasses, and all I saw were two blue irises and a set of dark pupils. I hoped that meant that while the sluagh were inside him, they weren't controlling him. "Why did you ask to see them?" he asked.

"When we were out in the sun, your eyes looked strange," I hedged. I didn't know if these monsters were listening to us, and I really didn't know what they were capable of. This wasn't the time or place to lay all of my cards on the table. "The sluagh avoided the sun, didn't they?"

"Those beasties? Aye, they kept to the shadows and the dark, as God's light could fair destroy them, being that they were unforgiven." Robert paused. "Why did you ask me that?"

"It's an interesting coincidence, with them not liking the light and it now bothering you. How did you destroy them, again?"

"I told you. I didn't destroy a single one of them. I helped them achieve forgiveness, and they moved on." Robert reached for me, and I moved to sit between his legs, with my torso against his chest. "I am feeling much better, love, though whether it's due to this rest or having you in my arms, I cannot say." He tightened his arms around me, and kissed the top of my head. "When I hold you, Karina my love, I feel like I can accomplish anything."

I pressed my cheek against his throat. He still smelled and felt and spoke like my Robert, but there was no telling how long this would last. I needed to figure out how to get these sluagh away from Robert, for good.

When we got home, I had to think fast. "Can you get started on some lunch for us?" I asked.

"Surely," Robert replied. "I'll just take stock of the larder."

"Great! I'll tell Chris," I said, then I barged into Chris's room. He was sitting on his bed with his computer on his lap, probably coming up with a few more awful book titles.

"We're not knocking before entering anymore, because?" he asked, without looking up.

"Robert's possessed."

Chris shut his laptop. "How do you know? And by what?"

"He can't bear sunlight," I began. "It's like he has a major hangover and can't take the bright light. But he doesn't have a hangover. I'm certain he doesn't, because I've been with him every day and we haven't had beer or anything alcoholic since last week."

"Even if he was hungover, it would hardly slow him down," Chris said. "He's got to be the healthiest person I've ever met." He put his laptop on the side table. I sat next to him on the bed. "What else happened?" When I hesitated, he added, "Obviously, you noticed something beyond light sensitivity."

"When I looked into his eyes, there was no reflection," I replied. "I expected to see myself, but I didn't. Instead, I saw a bunch of sluagh staring back at me."

Chris muttered a curse. "I thought Rob sent them back to Elphame."

"He told me forgave them, instead."

"Hm." Chris rubbed his chin. "How did he do that?"

I shrugged. "Something to do with holy water, and he was a minister back in the day. He probably sprinkled them, and poof! Possession."

"I wonder if the sluagh in his eyes are the same ones he forgave," Chris mused. "Perhaps they appreciated Rob's kindness, and they saw him as a leader. Maybe they chose to stay with him."

I recalled Robert's descriptions of how he'd rode at the head of the Wild Hunt. Always next to or right behind Nicnevin, and always with the host of Elphame stretched out behind him. To the sluagh, Robert must have been a mythical figure, not unlike Santa Claus, riding past them every winter.

"You may have a point," I said. "The sluagh don't seem to be doing anything malicious, either, aside from making him unusually sensitive to light."

"Then the sluagh are happy with Rob." Chris shook his head. "If they like hanging around with him, it's going to be awfully hard to get them to leave."

"What does their happiness have to do with anything?"

"Have you ever left a place you like, without having some sort of overriding reason?" he countered. "Take this cottage. We like it here, but our lives are in New York. Therefore, we're leaving."

"And the sluagh don't have any place else to go." I gazed across the common room to where Robert hunched over the kitchen counter, making sandwiches. Suddenly, he stopped what he was doing and rushed into the bedroom, and closed the door behind him.

"What was that about?" Chris asked.

"I have no idea," I replied, then Robert emerged from the room, sword out and wearing his armor.

"Karina, I have been summoned by the Seelie King," he declared. "I must go at once."

"Shit," I said.

Chris shook his head. "Shit indeed."

Back to Elphame

"I'm coming with you," Karina insisted, as she ran across the cottage toward me. "You'll need help!"

I stared at the woman, wondering what had put such an idea into her head. Allowing her to accompany me on this mission would do nothing save for endangering her life.

Then again, Karina was strong. I'd hiked with her across all sorts of terrain, and she never complained for the exertions, and I'd watched as she broke apart rocks both large and small to find those fossils she so adored. She'd also faced the Seelie Queen and won, which was a feat few could claim, myself included. Perhaps I would be a fool to tell her to remain behind.

"If you don't take her with you, she'll just figure out how to follow you," Christopher said, echoing my own thoughts. "You two might as well go together."

"All right," I said. "Be warned, love, I do not know what sort of creature we're about to face. For all I ken, this is a mission we'll not return from."

Karina took my hand. "Then we go down together. What do we need for preparations?"

I once wondered why I'd endured more than three hundred years as Nicnevin's prisoner. What had I done to earn such torment? I'd always strived to be a good man in both word and deed, and my reward had been centuries of torment in Elphame. Then Karina had freed me, my dearest love, with eyes that sparkled like the sky and the courage of a lioness, and I realized those lost centuries didn't matter. I would have waited another hundred or even a thousand years, just to touch her hand.

"Grab that field kit of yours, and fill the water bottles," I said. "Best to be prepared for whatever Elphame sees fit to throw at us."

Karina assembled her kit while Christopher put together rations that would be fit to travel. He ended up handing us a sack filled with that granola Karina was always snacking on, strips of dried meat, and two filled canteens.

"This should hold you for a day or two," he said; his hands trembled as he handed over the rations, and my heart went out to the lad. Being the elder sibling, Christopher saw himself as Karina's protector, but he couldn't return to Elphame with us. Not now, not when the injuries Nicnevin had inflicted upon him were still fresh in his mind, with the wounds hardly scabbed over. What he needed was time to heal.

I set my hand on his shoulder, and said, "I understand." His brow pinched, so I indicated his shaking hands with my gaze.

"Ah, yeah, I guess you would." He made a fist with one hand, and used the other to rub the back of his neck. "Just keep an eye out for Rina, okay?"

"Of course. I shall return her to you. Of that you have my word."

Christopher nodded, then Karina approached us with her geologist's kit strapped to her back. The items in the pack weren't the best defense against the horrors of Elphame, but needs must. "I'm ready if you are," she said.

I wasn't, not by any stretch of the imagination. However, it was best to not keep the king waiting. I took Karina's hands in mine, and said into the ether, "We are ready."

A moment later, we were in Elphame.

Forthright

The shift from Scotland to Elphame wasn't jarring, which was good. The last time Robert and I crossed dimensions, we'd jumped into a whirlwind—literally—and I was glad to learn that there was more than one way over. As for what the return trip would be like, I could only hope for a similarly smooth ride. With my luck, it would be anything but.

"Well, we're here," I said, because I just love stating the obvious. "Now what?"

"Now what, indeed." Robert sheathed his sword, and turned around in a slow circle as he observed our surroundings. We were in the center of a wildflower-studded field, the sun was shining overhead, and I could see what looked like a city or maybe a really large castle looming in the distance.

"This spot reminds me of *The Wizard of Oz*," I said. "All we need is a yellow brick road."

"Does this wizard reside near your home in Queens?" Robert asked.

"He's not a real guy. It's a story where an evil witch gets a house dropped on her, then her sister—the other evil witch—sends flying monkeys after the one responsible."

Robert grunted. "Let's hope we don't encounter any witches or monkeys."

"Agreed." The location really was beautiful. I brushed my hand against the wildflowers, then I remembered what had happened to

Dorothy and friends in the field of poppies. Beauty could be deceiving, especially in Elphame. "Do you know why the king sent us here?"

"'Tis something of a border dispute. That," he indicated the dark castle in the distance, "is Unseelie territory. According to the king, the Seelie border is being harried by a clutch of demons. The king would like them eradicated."

"Fionnlagh told you all of that?" During the few times I'd met the Seelie King, he'd been less than loquacious.

"His exact words were, 'Find the breach and destroy the demons,'" Robert replied.

"And we think these demons are Unseelie?" I asked, recalling the *fuath* that had hunted Robert and me through the streets of Crail. "What if they're more of Nicnevin's pets?"

"We shall learn more once we find them." He extended his hand to me. "Come, love. Let's move closer to the border, and attempt to learn about our foes."

I accepted his hand, and we walked toward the city in the distance. It was a beautiful day in Elphame, which was delightful and unusual. After being in Nicnevin's portion of the realm, which was so rotted it resembled an Otherworldly junkyard more than fairyland, I'd come to think of Elphame as a sort of hell dimension. The fact that we were enjoying an easy walk through a meadow on a sunny day was just odd.

Actually, that wasn't the only oddity.

"Why isn't the sun here bothering you here?" I asked. "At home, you could barely open your eyes when we were outside. Now, you're fine."

"I am not sure," he replied. "But you are correct. The blinding pain I felt earlier has all but disappeared."

"You were in pain?"

His frown told me he hadn't wanted to reveal that little detail. "Aye. It was like a group of horses were stampeding inside my head, all of them yearning to break free."

My throat tightened, and not only because Robert had been in such pain. Here we were, two people who'd pledged themselves to each other in every possible way, and we were keeping secrets. Worse, these secrets could get both of us killed. We both needed to do better, and that could start right now.

I stood in front of Robert, halting him. "I have to tell you something. Right before we took shelter in the caves near the beach walk, I looked in your eyes and saw a bunch of sluagh staring back at me."

Robert took a step back. "And you didn't think to tell me then?"

"You only just told me about your headache!"

"A headache is a damn sight different than seeing shades in my eyes," he retorted.

"I know, but when I saw them I didn't know if you were possessed, or what was going on," I replied, waving my arms around like a crazy person. "Then we got back to the cottage, and you went to make a sandwich, and before I could figure out what to do next, you put on your armor and said you were leaving!" I paused for breath. "We're not very good at communicating, are we?"

"No, we aren't," Robert admitted. "I want to be forthright with you in all things, but..."

"But?"

"Damn it, Karina, I also want to keep all of this from you," he said. "You were never meant to enter Elphame, or deal with any of the monsters here. You were meant to live a normal life, far from all of this." He looked away. "Far from a man like me."

"You weren't meant for this, either," I said. He nodded, but he wouldn't look at me. "Can you send your armor away? Just for a few minutes?"

Robert shook his head. "I don't think that is wise."

"I just want to hold you."

"Well, then." Before my eyes, his armor faded, and he was wearing a tee shirt and jeans. I slid my arms around his waist, and pressed my cheek against his chest. The terrors of Elphame faded away, and I was happy in his arms.

"I know we're still new to each other," I began. "And I know you've got trauma on top of trauma from everything Nicnevin put you through. But we need to be able to talk to each other. I'm sorry I didn't tell you about the sluagh when I first saw them. I thought I was protecting you, but I might have made it worse."

"Nothing is worse, for all that the information was delayed," Robert said. "Are you angry with me for forgiving, rather than destroying them?"

"No, I'm not," I said. "The fact that you could still try to help those monsters proves just how good you are, but it made me worry they were taking advantage of you. And that's why I had to come with you. What if the sluagh tried to hurt you again?"

Robert rested his forehead against mine. "You came here to protect me?"

"I know, it's silly," I began, then he tilted my chin up so he could meet my gaze.

"T'isn't. Not at all. Thank you, love, for looking out for me." His eyes searched mine. "What do you see in my eyes now?"

"Nothing. Just my reflection."

"Good." Robert tightened his arms around me, and for a moment, I just enjoyed holding him.

"Maybe the sluagh stayed behind in Crail."

"I doubt we would be that lucky," he began, then his body went rigid.

"What is it?" I demanded. "Is it your head? Are the sluagh back?"

"Not the sluagh." Robert stepped back, and his armor reappeared as he drew his sword. "I've seen something that could be what's been bothering the border."

I turned, and saw several dark forms slinking through the grass in the distance. "Are those panthers?"

"Cait sith," he replied. "They consume the souls of the newly dead."

"Then we're safe," I began, then I gasped. "But the sluagh are dead!"

"Aye, love, and we've no idea if they're still inside my head."

Cait Sith

As far as foes went, the cait sith were both beautiful and deadly.

They presented as smooth, sleek cats, with fur as black as night save for a white blaze across their breast, and eyes that reflected silver whenever they glanced in our direction. Even though they looked like animals now, but I'd seen them transform into a form that mirrored a human, and a warrior form that was somewhere between that of a man and cat. These were very dangerous creatures, and here Karina and I were, out in the open and with no cover to speak of.

"How do we fight these guys?" Karina asked. "Poisoned tuna?"

I smiled, for my beloved truly was fearless. "First, we need to ascertain if they truly are our foes. I would hate to start a row with the wrong individuals."

"Good point," she said. "How do we do that?"

"Asking should do, to start." I kept my sword out, and placed my other hand on my dirk as I strode toward the cait sith. "I am the gallowglass, and I have been sent here by the Seelie King," I called, once I was close enough. "He is concerned over the security of his lands."

The creature I assumed was the leader stood on his hind legs, and shifted form from cat to man. Beside me, I heard Karina gasp. "We were sent by his wife the queen, and for much the same reason," the cait said.

"I thought he was going to hiss, or meow," Karina whispered, and I struggled not to laugh. "But he sounds like a regular man."

"Not all monsters growl and hiss," I whispered back.

The cait, who apparently hadn't heard Karina's musings, continued, "Something has been wreaking havoc along the borderlands."

"Then we have a common foe." I found it odd that Fionnlagh and Nicnevin were both, and separately, interested in what was happening in the area, but I put that thought aside for the moment. It was hardly the oddest thing I'd ever encountered from the two of them. "Shall we work alongside one another?"

"Very well," the leader purred, then his gaze settled on Karina. "Why is the mortal here? Bait?"

"No," I replied. The caits did not need to know anything about Karina, not even her name. "Have you any idea what we're looking for?"

Another cait shifted to human form. That one was female. "We're not sure, but it comes over from the Unseelie lands," she said. "Every evening, the wraiths ride the winds here, and steal the Seelie bounty."

"Are they really wraiths?" Karina asked.

The female cait shrugged. "We'll know for certain once we find them."

Karina turned so the caits couldn't see her face, and whispered, "I don't like this. Do we believe these guys?"

"No," I said, then the male cait moved toward me. A heartbeat later, I realized he was staring hungrily at Karina. I grabbed her arm and dragged her away from him.

"Worry not," the cait said. "I never eat while on a mission."

"I thought they ate the souls of the dead," Karina said.

"They also hunt for fresh meat," I said.

I didn't let up my grasp on Karina's arm. My fingers were fair digging into her skin, and her grimace told me I was hurting her—only, this wasn't me. I felt the fear as surely as I felt Karina's arm under my hand, but it was not my fear. Times past when I'd been afraid it had been a blaze of shame that I'd done my best to douse with a feat of bravery. This fear was cold and hollow, and it wanted to pull me inside the darkness and hide away from the world.

This fear was that of the sluagh.

"Problem, gallowglass?" the cait taunted. "Not one to share, are you?"

"This fear, it's from my eyes," I muttered. "And what's taken up in them."

Karina's eyes widened, and I hoped she understood my meaning. She set her hand on mine, then she faced the cait.

"He's protective," she said. "And I'm not food."

"We'll see," the cait purred.

"Set your slimy paw or even a whisker on her, and your pelt will grace the floor in front of Nicnevin's hearth," I growled. "Will you show us where these wraiths have been sighted?"

"Of course," the cait said, seemingly unruffled by my threat. "Follow us."

The caits turned as one, and walked toward the Unseelie lands without waiting for our reply. The two who'd changed into human form led the way, but I heard the rest moving alongside us.

"Karina," I began, but she shook her head.

"Tell me later," she said, as she tapped the side of her head near her eye. Ah, then. She understood that my reaction had been influenced by the sluagh. "I don't think we're dealing with wraiths."

"Why is that?"

"Too easy," she replied. "Fionnlagh and Nicnevin could each handle a few wraiths on their own. Together, they would crush them. For Fionnlagh to send you, the threat must be something you can deal with better than he could."

Suddenly, the female cait was directly in front of Karina. "You think wraiths are an easy fight?" she purred.

"Probably not as easy as an overgrown kitten," Karina began, but I pushed her behind me. The cait watched, and laughed.

"Is that fear I smell?" she taunted. "Is the legendary gallowglass truly scared of little me? Or is your fear centered on what I might do to your mortal pet?"

"Have a care, a ghrá mo chroí," the male said, over his shoulder. "You heard her name."

The female looked Karina over as if she was a snack. "I could take her."

"You sure about that?" Karina countered, but the last thing we needed was to get into a literal cat fight.

"Enough," I said. "Run along to your pack, and don't try my patience."

The female sneered at me, but she returned to the leader's side. When she was a good distance ahead, I said, "They're a couple. He called her his beloved."

"I know."

"When did you start speaking Gaelic?"

"I only know the words you say to me," she replied. I considered what I usually murmured in her ear, and smiled.

"We'll have to vary our conversations," I said. "Your vocabulary's only fit for a brothel."

"Whose fault is that?"

I held out my arm. Karina fit herself alongside me, and for a moment we weren't surrounded by a pack of cait sith in Elphame, and I didn't have a host of sluagh taking up residence inside me. It was just her and I and our love.

"Despite our present circumstances, our life is good," I said.

Karina murmured her agreement, then she noticed something. "What's that?" she asked. "It's coming closer."

I turned to my right, and swore.

Redcaps

"Okay, based on that comment I guess these aren't the good guys?" I asked. Off in the distance was a group of creatures wearing bright red hats and carrying tall spears.

"Those creatures are redcaps, and no, they're not good," Robert replied. "The imps are little more than mercenaries."

"Why is the ground shaking?" I asked. I assumed that since Elphame was a magical dimension, it would be tectonically stable. Maybe they had volcanoes and tsunamis here, too. "Have you been through a lot of earthquakes here?"

"'Tis no earthquake. 'Tis the redcaps' boots," Robert replied. "They're shod in iron."

"That's... that's something." I couldn't imagine why anyone would want the excess weight of iron soles on their boots, then one singular reason came to mind. "Do they do that to ward off fairies?"

"More likely, they use the boots to sear their flesh when they stomp on them." Robert looked toward the cait leader. "Aye! Are you familiar with that lot?"

The cait had stopped moving, and watched as the redcaps approached us. I noticed his claws were out, and I giggled. The caits had retractable claws, just like housecats and kittens.

"They must be the wraiths we seek," the cait replied. "My pack shall circle behind." He made a quick motion with his hand, and the rest of the caits slunk away through the grass. "Nes, stand with me."

The female cait—Nes—stood beside her mate. Neither seemed afraid of the redcaps, which made me wonder if they all knew each other.

"This doesn't make any sense," I whispered to Robert. "They said we were after wraiths. I don't know much about redcaps, but they do not resemble wraiths. How could the caits make such a mistake?"

"If it was a mistake at all," Robert said. "Did you hear when the man warned his mate not to taunt you? He heard me say your name."

"What does my name have to do with anything?"

"Your name is now that of the one person to ever best Nicnevin in my lifetime," he replied. "Word travels fast, especially in Elphame."

"Great. Won't they be disappointed when they figure out I'm a geologist instead of a warrior." As I said the words, I reached into my pack and withdrew one of my picks. I didn't know if it would be a good weapon against a redcap, but all I had were picks and shovels.

I glanced at Nes and her mate. A pick might be a good weapon against a cait, if it came down to it.

"How do you feel?" I asked Robert, hoping he understood my true meaning. I didn't want to mention the sluagh, in case the caits had beef with them.

"I remain mildly terrified," he replied. "That in itself isn't unusual, for a man who faces a battle with no fear is a fool soon for the graveyard."

"You still get scared?"

"Aye, quite often."

I'd never thought of Robert as anything but fearless. We'd faced down some absolutely terrifying beasts, and he'd never shied away from any of them. If anything, his courage was the only thing that kept me from passing out from fright. But earlier, when the caits approached him, he'd backed up as if they were venomous snakes.

"What are you afraid of now?" I asked.

"Them," he replied, jerking his head toward the caits. "Although, I cannot explain why I am afraid of them."

"Have you encountered them before?"

"Many times. I've fought them, too, and was always victorious." He paused, and I wondered if any of those caits had challenged him in his role as gallowglass. He'd defeated every challenger he faced, and those deaths weighed heavily on him. "But this isn't fear of battle, or loss of life. This is terror, which is altogether new to me, and it seems to be caused by being as near to the caits as we are."

"Do you think you're feeling what *they* feel?" I asked, but Robert didn't get to reply. The redcaps were barreling toward us, and the last two caits had scattered. That meant the only targets left standing were Robert and me.

Crap.

"Behind me," Robert bellowed. I did as told, while he lowered his stance and held his shield in front of him. Amazingly, the charging redcaps split into two streams and flowed around us like water. Also, they were only about two feet tall.

"Why are their hats red?" I asked, as I clung to Robert's back, because being swarmed by tiny foes is a great time to discuss fashion.

"The imps dip their caps in the blood of their enemies," Robert replied. "The darker the red, the more kills to the wearer."

"That's so gross," I said, as a sea of bright red caps sailed past us. "I'm glad you never did that."

"Aye, you and me both."

Finally, all of the redcaps passed us. Robert lowered his shield, and turned to watch them.

"Where do you think they're going?" I asked.

"Truly, love, I've no notion." He glanced around the meadow, and continued, "The caits have vanished. Let's follow the redcaps, and hope the caits go in the other direction."

"The sluagh really are scared of the caits," I said, as we started after the redcaps.

"Aye, but it's not only that. There's something more afoot here than a border dispute."

"Sketchiness abounds in Elphame," I began, then the ground fell away from under my feet. I grabbed Robert's arms as we fell into a cavern below.

Darkness

I lay there, stunned, staring up at the hole in the ground. The ground had given way so fast we hadn't had a chance to scream. I reached for Karina, ignoring the dull ache in my shoulder, and the hundreds of sharp pains caused by the rock chips poking through the seams in my armor. My hand found Karina's back, felt it rise and fall, and I closed my eyes in relief. We were both alive. Everything else would work itself out.

"Karina," I murmured, as I gathered her against me. "Karina love, are you all right?"

"That was not fun," she said. "For our next trip, can we go somewhere quieter? A beach, maybe?"

I smiled as I pressed my lips against her forehead. If she was joking, she wasn't too badly hurt. "We visit the sea all the time."

"I meant a tropical beach. One that comes with mai tais."

"What is a mai tai?"

"It's a cocktail that tastes like pure happiness." She moved, patting my shoulder and chest with her hand, until her face was above mine. "Any idea where we are?"

"We should be able to get our bearings soon enough." I got to my feet, and surveyed the cavern. It extended farther than the eye could see in either direction. Toward my left, I heard the telltale gurgle of a stream.

"There's water that way," I said, pointing toward the sound. "Although, the ground is far steeper in that direction, and we don't know if the water is flowing into the cavern, or deeper into the earth. Best we stick to the flatter land away from the stream."

"How do you know where the ground is steep or flat?" Karina asked. "I can hear the water, but I can hardly see a thing."

"Are your eyes hurt?" I demanded, fearful she'd injured herself in the fall.

"My eyes are fine, but it's dark down here."

"Truly?" I could see as well as if it were daylight. "You can't see at all?"

"I can see a little from the light coming into the hole we came through, but that's it." She paused, and found my hand. "Are the sluagh helping you see in the dark?"

I opened my mouth to deny that such a thing was possible, then I recalled my terror over being near the caits, and my aversion to the earthly sun. "Perhaps they are influencing me more than I realized," I admitted.

Karina's fingers tightened on mine. "Robert, we're surrounded by rocks."

I heard the waver in her voice, and understood. "The sluagh will not harm you in any way," I declared. "If they try to make me throw something at you, I'll cut off my hand instead. I'll cut off my own head if I need to."

"If you do that, you'll be dead and I'll be stuck here alone," Karina said, then she placed her hand on my cheek. "Not that I don't appreciate you wanting to protect me."

I covered her hand with mine, and let my eyes close. Of course, me removing my head would do little to help Karina, and with the many fell deeds I'd committed, I would likely end up as an unforgiven shade myself. After all, that was probably why the sluagh had been drawn to me in the first place, for like does attract like.

Setting those dark thoughts aside, I probed the depths of my mind. The terror I'd felt when we were close to the caits had abated, and I felt nothing but love for Karina, and a mild concern about finding our way out of the cavern. Perhaps the sluagh had given up on their dislike of her, which made me wonder if I could convince the shades to help us.

"When I spoke with the sluagh, they told me they tormented you because they thought you were the reason I was no longer in Elphame," I began. "I made it clear that I had left Elphame of my own free will, and that harming you in any way would only cause me to eradicate them permanently."

"And then you forgave them?"

"Aye. I did. They'd committed several misdeeds, that is true, but it's not for me to judge another's soul. However, even though they'd done evil things, and even though they'd harmed you, I couldn't turn my back on those in need."

"You're a good man," Karina said. "You know that."

I kissed her forehead. "Love helps one do the right thing."

"It sure does, but I am glad you told them to leave me alone." She was silent for a time. "I have a theory."

"Please. Share it with me."

"I think you're the first person who showed the sluagh kindness in a long time. Possibly ever. And because of that, I'm wondering if they see you as their leader."

"Leader?" I repeated. "Then why are they possessing me?"

"Are they? Or are they just hitching a ride?"

I paused, considering Karina's words. If the sluagh did see me as a leader, why were they inside my head instead of marching beside me? Then again, they might not have had any other way to follow me, especially during the day. But now, we were in a deep, dark cave, and it was time for them to travel under their own power and not mine.

"Karina, I believe you are correct." I stood, and drew my sword. "And this free ride ends now."

Caves

Robert loomed over me, a hulking figure in the dark cavern. His sword's edge caught the dim light and somehow magnified it, illuminating his face and torso. Then he raised his sword, and boomed, "Unforgiven dead! Shades of the damned! I demand you appear before me!"

Three glowing trails of smoke manifested around Robert. Slowly, they coalesced into the same monsters that had thrown rocks at me on a sunny day in the village. "Robert, the rocks," I reminded him.

"You gave me your word no harm would come to Karina," Robert declared. "Keep your promises, and I will keep mine. Do not make me regret forgiving you!" The wraiths quivered, but that was all they did. "Do I make myself clear?"

"Yes," they wailed as one. "We shall love Karina as we love you."

"We don't need you to love either one of us," I said. "Just don't be murderous and we'll get along fine."

When the sluagh wailed louder, Robert said, "Silence, please." Once they'd quieted down, he continued, "Why are you hanging on to me?"

"You helped us," the sluagh replied. "We want to help you in return, but we don't know how."

"Attaching yourself to my body is not the way," Robert said.

"Definitely not," I said. "But since they want to help us, I have an idea."

"What would you have them do?" Robert asked.

"Since they're made of shadows, can they affect the shadows down here?" I asked. "You know, maybe lighten things up so we can see where we're going."

"A sound plan," Robert said. "I will say, now that they're separate from me, I can't see my hand in front of my face in this gloom." He paused, and said, "Go on. Ask. It's your idea."

"Um. Okay." I turned to where I thought they were hovering, and asked, "Sluagh, can you help us get around in the dark? Or maybe make it less dark?"

When nothing happened, Robert said, "From now on, you will obey Karina as you would obey me. Now can you draw back the shadows, or no?"

The sluagh remained silent, but the darkness around us shimmered like an oil slick hanging in mid-air. Then, the darkness moved.

"Robert, what's happening?" I asked.

"Here." He wrapped his arm around my shoulders, and raised his shield in front of us. "I've got you."

I turned so my face was pressed against his armored chest. I trusted Robert, but I had no idea what the sluagh were trying. For all I knew they were using the darkness as cover to fire up a tornado of rocks to send directly at us. The air swirled around us, and the shadows took on a life of their own. It was like we were trapped in the world's worst puppet show. My fears got the better of me, and I closed my eyes.

"Amazing," Robert whispered. I cracked an eyelid, and saw that he was holding a smooth black orb.

"Is that obsidian?"

"No," he replied. "It's the darkness."

Gingerly, I touched the orb. It appeared solid, but felt warm and pliable. As I marveled at the orb, I realized how well I could see it. There was no darkness in the cavern, and while it wasn't illuminated with sunlight, no shadows obscured my vision. Incredibly, Robert held all of the shadows in his hand.

"This is not what I expected." I pressed on the orb. It yielded, but only just. Its behavior reminded me of nothing so much as a water balloon. I glanced up, and saw the sluagh hovering in front of us. "Thank you."

"We will do as you say," the sluagh said as they swirled around us. "We will obey."

"Now that that's sorted," I muttered. "Should we try to get out of here?"

"Aye," Robert murmured. "But which way?"

"Who's in charge of the redcaps?" I asked, since I felt we needed that question answered first. "The caits didn't like them, and I feel like the caits are bad news. Maybe we should be on Team Redcap." The sluagh began keening when I mentioned the caits. Nice to know we were in agreement about those furballs.

"The caits are loyal to Nicnevin, which is not an endorsement to their character," Robert said. "As for the redcaps, as far as I ken they've always kept to themselves. Even they don't lower themselves to serve the Unseelie."

"But the Unseelie aren't bad, just different, right?" I pressed. "And what do you mean, as far as you know? You're the expert here."

"I am somewhat knowledgeable about the imps, but I've encountered them only a handful of times. According to most of the lore, redcaps cannot stand to be in the presence of God. They cannot abide being inside a kirk, or even hearing a few lines of verse."

"And you being a minister made you redcap proof," I concluded, recalling how the swarm of redcaps had avoided all contact with Robert. "So why did they show up at all?"

"Do you think they were sent to intercept us?"

"I don't know. But it's weird, what with us encountering the caits and then the redcaps barreling over everyone. Like you said earlier, it seems like there's more going on than just a border dispute."

Robert grunted, then he turned to the sluagh. "I want two of you to find the redcaps that marched past us earlier, determine who or what is issuing their orders, and report back to us as soon as possible," he began. "As for the one who remains with us, Karina and I need to find our way out of this cavern. Stay with us, reduce the shadows, and help us find a way out. And if any of you even think of tossing a rock or pebble or even a harsh glance toward my beloved, I will not be pleased," he added.

"Yes, master," the sluagh whispered, then two of the wraiths dissipated.

"I'm your beloved?" I asked Robert, only because I wanted to hear his answer.

"You ken that well," he replied. "Now, let's find our way back to the surface."

We walked for a time. The sluagh remained true to its word, and kept the darkness around us at bay. If I'd been stuck in one of Elphame's caves at any other time, I'd be fascinated, and taking as many specimens and notes as possible. What if I found fossils in fairyland? Now that would be the best scientific discovery in the history of discoveries... but this was Elphame. For all we knew, this cave was home to creatures who would find Robert and me exceedingly tasty.

"Are there other caverns in Elphame?" I asked.

"Aye, though I've been in very few of them," Robert replied. "Underground and in the dark in not a good place for a battle, you ken." He paused, and asked, "But you like it here, don't you?"

"I like the rocks, but I wish we were on the surface," I said. "If we ever come back to these caves, maybe we can bring some flashlights, and grab a few samples for my collection."

"I'll make certain we do."

Eventually, we reached a crack in the rocks. Orange and gold light streamed into the cave; it must be near sunset.

"There is the exit," the sluagh hissed. "A village lies to the east. Shall I accompany you?"

"Find the other two, and report back to us once you're all together," Robert ordered. "We shall await you in the village."

As soon as the sluagh faded from view, I asked, "Any idea what's in this village?"

"None at all," he replied. Honesty was nice, but not always reassuring. "However, most villages in Elphame resemble those from my youth, at least superficially. We should encounter a market, along with an inn, and perhaps a smithy."

"Are there a lot of villages in Elphame?"

"Aye, especially here in the borderlands," Robert said. "These areas tend to be somewhat insulated from the goings on of the higher courts."

"Then it's even weirder that the caits and redcaps are here," I said. "Maybe the villagers will know something about these border troubles."

"That they might. Whether or not they share it with us is something else entirely."

The Village Inn

Soon enough, we saw the village in the distance. It was a good size, and I hoped the inn was serving something palatable to humans. However, there was the matter of how we would pay for our lodgings.

"I have some money," Karina said, when I shared my concerns. "And we have all that granola to eat, too."

"Unless you've got gold in one form or another, your money's all but useless in Elphame," I replied. I did not mention the granola, mostly because I would rather starve than eat that dried mess. "Most don't even have what we would consider money."

"Then how do people pay for goods and services around here?" Karina asked. "Barter?"

"Essentially, yes," I replied. "We shall inquire what needs doing around the inn, and trade labor for lodging. Perhaps I will chop some wood in trade for a room, or act as a farrier."

"I don't know about that," Karina said. "When was the last time you put a shoe on a horse?"

"It's not like the process has changed," I said, instead of answering her question. However, she had a point. All horses would be better off without the likes of me poking at their hooves.

"All right," Karina said. "Let's ask the innkeeper what a room's worth these days."

"A moment." I sent my armor and sword into the fath fidh. There they would remain, safe and out of sight until I had need of them again. "I'd rather not be revealed as the gallowglass, at least not right away."

"Makes sense," she said, then she withdrew a plaid shawl from her pack and wrapped it around her shoulders. The shawl didn't completely obscure her modern clothing, but it helped her blend in a bit more. "We'll pretend we're looking for some land of our own, and who knows? Maybe this inn has a pitcher of mai tais in the back."

I must find a recipe for this beverage that made Karina smile as bright as the sun. "I suppose anything is possible."

We entered the village, and walked through the marketplace on our way to the inn. The market stalls bustled with activity, and I was pleased that no one paid too much attention to Karina and me. Also, many of the denizens appeared to be human. That told me I was right to send my armor away. Hopefully, we could blend in with the locals, and most would assume we were mere travelers.

"Check out all these kilns," Karina said, as she pointed toward a cluster of low brick structures just visible beyond the market stalls. "They must make a lot of pottery here. Although, I don't see any being sold."

"Perhaps it's made for local use," I suggested. Karina nodded, but didn't look convinced. While I trusted her instincts, I wasn't too concerned with the village's pottery wares.

The inn itself was a grand affair. It was two levels high, with a wattle and daub exterior, and topped with a freshly thatched roof. When we stepped inside the common room, we were greeted with the warm smells of baking bread and roasted meat. This was the sort of place I could spend days in, relaxing without a care in the world.

"Nice place," Karina said. "Who do we talk to about getting a room?"

I spied who I assumed was the innkeeper behind the bar. "Good evening," I greeted, as I strode toward the bar. "Have you a room for two weary travelers?"

"We surely do," he replied. "We haven't been getting many travelers these days, what with the unrest in the borders."

"Oh?" I asked. "What seems to be happening?"

"Something is stealing the ore from the mines," he replied. "No one is certain how it's happening, but the dwarves are up in arms. Word is they've called on the local redcaps for assistance."

That answered one of our questions, and raised several more. "Have the redcaps scared away the bulk of your business?" I asked.

"The redcaps are our saving grace," the innkeeper replied. "The entire demesne relied on those mines, and without the ore to trade, we may starve in our very homes."

"My apologies," I said, as I tipped my head toward him. "I meant no offense, only to understand."

"No offense taken," he said, then he poured two mugs of ale for myself and Karina. "What brings you to this corner of Elphame?"

"My bride and I seek a plot of land," I replied. "We wish to build a home, and begin our family."

"We do?" Karina squeaked.

"The sooner the better," I said, as I pulled her toward me. Perhaps I should have warned her before mentioning children, even in jest. "Our fondest wish is to fill a home with children."

"Such good news," the innkeeper said, as Karina stepped on my foot. "It's been too long since we had new crofters. Where shall you stay in the meantime?"

"Perhaps in one of your fine rooms," I said, as I gestured to encompass the whole of the inn. "I'm a hard worker, and can earn our keep."

The innkeeper shook his head. "I would love to strike such a bargain, but since we have few guests therefore there isn't much work to be offered."

"Maybe we don't need to work," Karina said. "What sort of ore is being stolen from the mines?"

"Iron, of course," he replied. "It's the only substance known to keep the evil fae at bay."

Karina rooted around in her pack, and produced a battered iron chisel. "This is iron. Is it worth enough for us to have a room for tonight?"

The innkeeper stared at the chisel, as if it was a trick and not a solid piece of metal. Eventually, he picked it up, feeling the weight of it.

"This is a fine piece of iron, and worth much more that a night's rest," he said. "This piece is worth a fortnight's room and board for the both of you. How did you come by it?"

"I've had it for years," she replied. "I use it to break apart rocks, and study what's inside."

"What's inside," the innkeeper murmured, and I hoped Karina hadn't made a mistake. If this village truly coveted iron, she could have inadvertently placed a target on our heads. I'd no sooner formed the thought when the innkeeper smiled.

"How serendipitous that you both have happened by our village," he said, as he stashed the chisel in his apron. "Have you a horse needing to be put up?"

"We don't," I replied.

"With this amount of metal, we might be able to secure you a pair," he said. "You're certain you're willing to part with the iron?"

"I am," Karina replied. "We need the room, and you need the iron. I'd call that a good trade."

"Yes," the innkeeper said, as his gaze lingered on Karina's pack. "Quite a good trade."

Here

The innkeeper, who we discovered was called Rudrick, led us upstairs to our room, clutching my battered old chisel the entire time. I probably should have offered him my newer, nicer chisel that had only been used in the field once. However, that one time had been when Robert and I went prospecting for fossils in Dob's Linn, and it had sentimental value.

I also didn't like the way Rudrick was eyeing my pack. Reading minds wasn't something I could do, but I was willing to bet he wanted to know if I had any more iron on me. The last thing I needed was to produce more metal, and seem like I was the inn's new piggy bank. Better for Rudrick to think he'd swindled me out of all of my iron, and leave it at that.

"Here we are," Rudrick said, as he opened a door on the second floor. "These are the best rooms we offer. There's a sitting room, bedchamber, and the stairs in the back corner lead to the hot spring below."

"A hot spring," I repeated. "Does everyone in the inn have access to it?"

"They do," Rudrick replied, "but you're our only guests tonight. If privacy is what you're after, I'm sure you'll find plenty."

"This room shall do nicely," Robert said. "Many thanks, my friend."

"Of course. I'll send up a girl with your supper. Until then, rest well." With that, Rudrick shut the door behind him. I dropped my pack on the small table in the center of the room, and went to investigate a tall wooden cupboard. It turned out to be filled with neatly folded linens.

"Interesting," I murmured.

"What were you hoping to find in there?" Robert asked.

"I'm not sure," I replied. "I've never been in an old-fashioned inn before. This is all new to me." I stepped into the bedchamber. The walls were hung with red and gold tapestries, and the room was dominated by a four-poster bed topped with a lacy white canopy. "This is so cool."

Robert stood behind me, and wrapped his arms around my shoulders. "I'm glad you're pleased with our accommodations."

"You've been in rooms like this a billion times, haven't you?"

"Not quite a billion, but many times," he replied, dipping his head to kiss my neck. "But this is the first time I've been in a room like this with you. Therefore, this is the most special time of all of them."

He always said the best things. "What do you want to check out first? Bed, or hot spring?"

A knock sounded at the door. "I expect that will be our supper," Robert said, then he admitted a serving girl carrying a full tray. I'd wondered what sort of creatures worked at the inn, but she appeared to be as human as Rudrick. Which, of course, didn't mean she was human, but at least she wasn't a cait or a redcap. That made her okay in my book.

I moved my pack from the table into the bedroom, then we helped her unload the many plates and bowls. As soon as she left, we started on our supper. There were meat pies, a tureen of stew, and not one but two loaves of bread. There was even a pitcher of ale to wash everything down.

"I can't believe how good everything is," I said, as I started on my third meat pie. They were small, which was how I justified eating pie number three. It was also how I'd justified my second bowl of stew. "Do you think they have a magic cook?"

"I suspect the answer's far more mundane," Robert replied. "In my experience, simple food made by simple people tends to sit better than rich fare."

"I think you're right." I set down my half eaten pie. "And I'm stuffed."

"Bath before bed?" he asked, with a glint in his eye.

"Definitely." I pushed back from the table and opened the linen cupboard. "If you take care of locking the door, I'll find us something to use as bathrobes."

Robert was more successful in his task than I was. The main door to our room had a lock, but we didn't have the key, which was unusual but not a deal breaker. He ended up barricading the door with the table and chairs. It wasn't that we didn't trust Rudrick—we were suspicious, yes, but not outright distrustful—but better safe than sorry. As for our robes, the cupboard only contained linen sheets, so we descended to the hot springs looking like Roman senators decked out in our best togas.

"Careful, love," Robert said, when I almost lost my footing on the stone steps. The steam from the springs made everything slippery.

"I'm okay," I said, then I stepped onto the ground floor and gasped. The roof of the cavern was covered with softly glowing crystals in shades of purple and green. The hot spring itself emptied into a deep blue pool. Steam rose from the surface of the water, making lacy designs in the air.

"The ceiling is phosphorescent rock," I said. "It must be calcite, or maybe fluorite." I glanced at Robert. "These rocks would have been useful in the caves."

"Aye, they would have." He reached up and touched one of the glowing stones. "I wonder what makes them glow?"

"If we were home, I'd say there's an ultraviolet light source nearby. Here, it's probably magic." Tentatively, I dipped my toes in the water. It was the perfect temperature. "I hope there isn't a sea monster in there."

"Doubtful," Robert said, as he shed his makeshift toga. The gentle glow from the ceiling illuminated the planes and swells of his muscles in all the right ways. "We're rather far from the sea."

Laughing, I dropped my sheet and followed Robert into the water. Moving through the pool was like swimming through warm honey, and by the time we reached the far side, my muscles were liquid. There was a bench carved into the living rock, and we sat next to each other.

"Sometimes, Elphame doesn't seem so bad," I said.

Robert laughed deep in his chest. "Aye, love. Much like our world, there's pleasure and pain in equal measures."

I leaned against the cave wall, enjoying Robert's laughter. Thanks to his time as the gallowglass, he was always on alert for anything out of the ordinary. It was rare for him to relax, even when it was just the two of us. But now, here in a hot spring beneath an inn with our bellies full of stew and meat pies, he let the hypervigilant assassin go, and he was just Robert.

I absolutely adored him.

Slowly, because the last thing I wanted to do was startle him, I moved to sit on his lap with my legs curled around his waist, my heart beating close to his. His eyes remained closed, but his hands steadied my lower back. The steam had made the curls in his dark hair tighten into ringlets. I attempted to tally the water droplets on his lashes, and lost count.

"You're so pretty," I murmured. Again he laughed, a deep rumble that did things to me.

"In all the time I've been alive," he said, as his hands slid down to my hips, "no one has ever called me pretty."

"Well then," I said, as I lifted myself up, "they weren't looking at you properly."

"Is that so," he murmured. I felt the blunt head of his cock pressing against me. "Here?"

"Here," I said, then I slid onto him. Robert kissed my neck as I began to move. We quickly found our rhythm, and I don't know if it was due to our exhaustion or the beauty of the cave or what, but neither one of us lasted long.

Afterward, I laid against Robert's chest soaking in the afterglow, literally and figuratively. The crystals' glow had darkened to a bluish purple, and Robert was still half hard inside me. As I laid against him, feeling his heartbeat, I never wanted to move.

"Karina," Robert murmured, as his fingers danced down my spine. "Truly, my beloved, I have never felt the way I do with you. You are the other half of my heart."

"Really?" I murmured, sounding far needier than I'd intended. But Robert had been married twice, and his love for his first wife was the stuff of legend. "Even though—"

He kissed me before I could finish my question. "Even though," he said against my lips. "Karina, mo chroí, tha gaol agam ort."

"I love you too."

Thief

After our sojourn in the hot spring, Karina and I tumbled into bed and slept as if we hadn't a care in the world. I only woke once during the night, and found Karina lying against me with her cheek resting over my heart. As I stroked her hair back from her face, I wondered what she dreamed about. Was it more of those rocks and fossils that fascinated her so, or did she dream of her future? Perhaps she was drawn to a time when her schooling would be complete, when she was settled into her chosen path. I wondered if she ever dreamed of me.

For the longest time, I thought I'd lost the ability to dream. After Nicnevin captured me, my dreams were more like memories of a time when I wasn't the gallowglass, long before I'd ever killed a man or a monster. Then Karina freed me from the tree I'd been imprisoned in atop Doon Hill, and that very night I dreamt of a woman with a sparkling eyes and a gentle laugh. The images in my dream were like ripples on a pond, and when they settled I realized that woman was none other than Karina. When I woke the next morning, I desired nothing more than to learn everything about her.

And now she slept in my arms, my perfect lass, my dream come true. I kissed her forehead, and let myself drift off to sleep.

When next I woke, it was because someone was picking the lock to our door.

"Stay here," I said to Karina, as my armor covered me and my sword appeared in my hand. I stalked out to the front room and shoved the barricade aside, and flung open the door. The thief, hunched over in the dark corridor, dropped his tools and tried to run, but I grabbed him by the scruff of his neck.

"Thieves are truly the most foolish of people," I growled. "You made so much noise picking that lock, you woke me up. What's more, the lock wasn't even engaged." When the thief did nothing but whimper, I shook them. "Have you anything to say for yourself?"

"You gave Rudrick that nice slab of iron," she whispered. "I thought you might have more."

The female voice surprised me. I thought I'd grabbed a boy who needed to be scared out of a life of thievery. "And you thought stealing was the best way to get some for yourself?" I demanded.

"Robert," Karina said, as she turned up the lamps. She'd wrapped herself up in one of the linen sheets again, and was standing very close to the flames. I hoped a stray thread wouldn't catch fire. "It's the girl from earlier, who brought us supper."

That complicated things, mainly because it meant the innkeeper may not be trustworthy. I dropped her into one of the chairs, and asked, "Did Rudrick send you to rob us?"

"No," she said, shaking her head. "Rudrick would never. But we've had so little ore of late, and we're hungry."

"Do you eat the iron?" Karina asked.

"Of course not," she replied. "But it's all we have of value. Without the ore to trade, I don't know what will become of us."

Karina and I shared a look. Her frown spoke volumes. "What's your name?" I asked the girl.

"Mare," she replied. "You're not going to tell Rudrick about this, are you?"

"I haven't decided," I said. An innkeeper needed to know if he had a thief on his payroll, but if hunger had truly driven Mare's actions, I didn't want to punish her further. "However, if you're willing to help Karina and I with our mission, perhaps we can come to an agreement."

Mare looked at her hands. "I'm not sure I can," she said. "I'm only a kitchen girl."

"And the best gossip always comes from the kitchen," Karina said, as she sat in the chair across from Mare. "Can I ask you a few questions?"

The girl nodded.

"What do you know about the mining process?" Karina asked. "As in, who's digging up the ore, refining it, stuff like that."

"The dwarves control all the mines in the area," Mare began. "It's not a bad thing, since no one besides them really wants to spend all day underground breaking rocks. Every week the dwarves would bring a cartful of ore to the guildhall, and they would distribute it in exchange for what they needed."

"What do dwarves need?" Karina asked.

"Food, ale, boots," Mare rattled off. "Things like that."

"So you—the villagers—traded with the dwarves for ore," Karina said, and Mare nodded. "Who refined it?"

"We had a guild of metalworkers," Mare said. "Around here, you either work with metal, or you work with the people who trade for the metal. Everything went on that way for years, then the metalworkers began dying."

"Dying?" Karina repeated. "We're they old, or sick?"

"No," Mare said, wide eyed and terrified. "Their throats were slit, each and every one of them. And each of them had been robbed of the iron they'd been working."

"Did you know these metalworkers well?" Karina asked, gently.

"Yes," Mare whispered. "I knew them very well. We all did."

Karina glanced at me. I moved to stand beside her, then I said to Mare, "I am very sorry for your loss. Truly, that is an awful way to go." Mare nodded, and choked down a sob. "Forgive me for inquiring about such a gruesome detail, but do you know how the deed was done?"

"No one does," she replied. "But each murder was done the same way, with a slash across the throat. I saw a few of them. It looked like a wild animal had done it, but there are no animals nearby with such large claws."

Claws. "Thank you for telling me that, Mare. I know that can't have been easy." I was about to send the girl on her way, but Karina had more questions.

"Was it the refined metal, or the ore that was stolen from the metalworkers?" Karina asked.

"It was the finished metal only," Mare replied. "Now that the metalworkers have all gone, the dwarves are refusing to bring us any more ore until more metalworkers come to work for us, but why would they do that when all the rest were murdered? The dwarves have even gotten in with the redcaps to help guard their mines. They're afeared someone will steal the ore from right under their noses, and then where would we be?"

Karina patted Mare's forearm, then she said to me, "Refined iron is a very different substance than the raw ore. Whoever's doing this wasn't after the iron. They wanted this village to stop refining it, and lose their main source of revenue in the process."

"How do you know so much about iron?" Mare asked. "Are you a metalworker?"

"Not quite," Karina replied. "I'm a geologist, which means I specialize in rocks. However, iron ore exists when the metal is embedded inside certain rocks, so I understand its properties." She frowned, and added, "Will Rudrick be safe, being that I gave him a piece of iron?"

"Rudrick knows better than to show off," Mare replied. "I only know about it because I was behind the bar when the trade happened."

Karina grinned. "Like I said, the ones in the kitchen always know what's really going on."

Mare returned her smile, then she looked up at me. "Are you also a scholar?"

"Aye, but these days I serve the Seelie King," I replied.

"Have you come to save us, then?"

"Yes, Mare," I replied. "Yes, we have."

Refining the Ore

Robert sent Mare on her way while I got dressed, and thought about what we'd just learned. The village's main trade good was refined iron, and now that the metalworkers were all dead, they had a surplus of the raw ore and no way to process it. It was a recipe for disaster, except for the fact that it was rather easy to extract iron from the ore. You crushed the rock as finely as you could, then added the product to an amazingly hot furnace, and the pure iron melted away. It was hard, hot work, but easy enough to accomplish, especially if your only options were refine or starve. If I was in this situation, I would have started stoking those furnaces right away, instead of waiting for random travelers to show up with used chisels.

"Why would someone want to harm this village?" I asked Robert, as I joined him in the front room. He'd re-barricaded the door, and was checking the room's sole window.

"You think the village as a whole is the target, not just the iron mines?" he asked.

"According to Mare, there's plenty of ore left in the mines." I shook my head. "I don't think this has anything to do with the Unseelie sneaking across the borders. Not directly, anyway."

Robert rubbed his chin. "What of the sluagh?"

"What about them?" I began, then I paused. "They showed up and tried to drive us apart, but then they ended up helping us. I don't think that's a coincidence. Maybe someone thought we would need their help."

"Who would send the sluagh on a mercy mission?"

I shrugged. "Nicnevin? She's as nutty as a fruitcake. I wouldn't put anything past her."

"Nor would I." Robert picked up the mass of shadows the sluagh had collected in the cave, and stashed it inside his armor. "What should we do next?"

"I'd like to take a look at these refineries."

Robert agreed with my plan. Since we hadn't traveled to Elphame with much, we brought it all with us when we left our room. The place had already been the subject of an attempted break in, and I didn't need anyone stealing my favorite backpack. Once we were outside the inn, I turned around and regarded the building.

"Something's off about Rudrick, too," I murmured. "He was awfully helpful, even before I gave him the chisel. I feel like everything that's happened over the past few days was engineered to lead us right here."

Robert grunted. "I do not appreciate being treated like a puppet, and having others pull my strings."

"Neither do I." I spotted a brick structure in the distance. Yesterday I'd thought the brick structures were kilns, but now I was hoping it was one of the refineries. As I began walking toward it, I asked, "Back when you rode with the Wild Hunt, and you helped round up the sluagh, what happened to them afterward?"

"They went into Fionnlagh's care," he replied. "In exchange for their fealty, he offered them a new life in Elphame."

"Interesting. Did the sluagh know this beforehand?"

"No. The offer was only made after the Hunt returned to court." We walked in silence for a few moments. "You're wondering if Nicnevin sent the sluagh to harass you, rather than to help us."

"The thought had crossed my mind." We reached the brick structure, and learned my hunch was correct. "This is what's called a bloomery furnace, which means the ore was refined here."

"Is that so." Robert walked all the way around the furnace, then he gave the bellows a push. Cold black ash scattered around the base of the furnace. "After the metalworkers put the ore through the furnace, how would the iron reveal itself?"

"The metal would melt and fall to the bottom." Using my foot, I indicated the opening at the bottom of the furnace. "You'd have to wait a while for it to cool off, then you could do whatever you wanted with it."

Robert nodded, then he looked toward the village. "And there is the closest smithy. That's where the next steps in the process would occur."

I followed Robert's gaze, then I saw a low wooden structure with its own brick furnace built into the side. It was on the far side of the inn from the entrance, so we hadn't seen it when we entered last night. "Looks like Rudrick has a smith on staff."

"I am beginning to think Rudrick is not merely a kindly innkeeper," Robert said.

"He's definitely sketchy." We went around the back of the inn and entered the smithy. The blacksmith wasn't present, which was nice. What was present were racks and racks of wooden spears, all of them devoid of their metal tips. "I guess we know what they were making," I said, as I ran my fingers across the smooth black shafts.

"I've seen these spears before," Robert said. "These are used by the Unseelie army. What with the iron only being in the spear's tip, they can wield them without harming themselves."

"Unseelie spears. But we're in Seelie territory," I said.

"Aye, love, that we are. Which means whomever is crafting these spears for the Unseelie is breaking Fionnlagh's laws."

I heard movement behind me. Expecting to see Rudrick or maybe Mare, I turned and saw the caits' leader leaning against the doorframe. His claws were out, wickedly sharp curves that caught the light like ten tiny blades. "Perhaps Fionnlagh's laws need to be broken now and then."

Master of Shadows

I stepped in front of Karina as I drew my sword. "How is Nicnevin involved in all of this?" I demanded.

The cait shrugged. "Is she?"

"You said you were sent by her!"

"So trusting, gallowglass," said the female cait, Nes, as she slunk around her partner and stepped inside the room. "I wonder if Karina ever takes advantage of your sweet naïveté?"

Karina hefted the smith's hammer, and said, "Come closer and ask me that again."

The caits hissed, and I widened my stance. I was confident I could handle them both and defend Karina, although if my beloved wanted to beat Nes senseless, I certainly wouldn't get in her way. Then I heard rustling in the thatched roof above us. I looked up, and saw a dozen sets of eyes staring down through the thatch.

"Karina," I murmured. "We are surrounded."

She glanced upward, and uttered a few words that no woman would have said back in my youth. "How many can you take?"

I didn't respond, because it was no longer about how many caits I could defeat on my own. The caits knew that Karina was my weakness, and while I could easily rout this lot, there were too many for me to fight while defending Karina at the same time. I couldn't risk a fight where she might be harmed.

The caits began tearing the roof apart and dropping into the smithy. Suddenly, I couldn't risk not fighting them any more than I could risk rushing at them pell mell. I needed something to either distract or incapacitate the caits immediately, then I recalled the globe of shadows.

I withdrew the globe, and threw it at the caits feet. "Shadows, disperse," I ordered. The globe shattered, and the smithy was engulfed in blackness. I heard the caits screeching and hissing, but not retreating.

Karina put her hand on my arm. I passed her my dirk.

"This way," I said. Sword up, I inched toward where I recalled the door was in relation to the room. Claws raked across my armor, and I shouldered past the creature. My goal was leaving the smithy altogether, and letting the caits fight among themselves in the darkness. Then Karina shrieked and my blood went cold.

"Karina!"

"I'm okay," she replied. "Keep moving!"

I did, and half a dozen steps later we were outside. As I turned back, I saw three deep gouges on Karina's arm.

"They hurt you?" I growled.

She held up my dirk. There was blood on the blade. "I hurt them back."

I nodded, satisfied for now. As for the smithy, the darkness was contained inside. The windows and doorway were covered with a shining blackness, not unlike obsidian.

One of the sluagh appeared in front of me. "Command the shadows to thicken," it rasped. "Trap them inside."

"Why can't you do that?" I asked.

"You released the shadows," it replied. "You are their master."

I stared at the wraith, wondering how that could be possible. I'd wielded magic before, but only as it related to my weapons and armor. Then a crash came from within the smithy, and a cait howled. The time for contemplation was over.

I faced the smithy's door, and yelled, "Thicken!"

The darkness in the windows and doors went from obsidian's shine to tar's dull glow as the noises from within went from angry to panicked. The caits were trapped, for now.

Karina slumped against me. I glanced down, and saw her wound freely bleeding. "We need to bandage your arm."

"We also need to talk to Rudrick again." She pushed off from me, and began walking toward the front of the inn. "Since you can wield shadows now, should everyone call you the shadowglass?"

"I wield naught but my sword."

"The shadows from the cave are now beholden to you," the sluagh murmured. "They shall do your bidding until light obliterates them."

"What happens when they're obliterated?" I asked.

"They cease to be."

"Hear that, shadowglass?" Karina asked. "Now you've got a herd of shadows to watch over."

I narrowed my eyes at this woman I adored with my whole heart. "Let's get your arm seen to, and worry about the shadows afterward."

"As you say, Duke of Darkness."

"Karina!"

"Sultan of Shadows?" She paused. "Is there a word for darkness that starts with p? So you could be the Preacher of..."

"Keep it up, and I will suggest all of these as titles to Christopher for his next book."

She gasped. "You wouldn't!"

I glanced at her, intending to tease her a bit more, only to frown when I saw her wounded arm. While I enjoyed our banter, my primary concern was seeing to Karina's injury. Once she was comfortable, our next order of business would be questioning the innkeeper. And his answers had best be truthful.

Know Better, Do Better

As soon as we entered the inn, we went straight to the kitchens. There I found my new friend, Mare, kneading dough.

"Mistress, what happened?" she asked when she saw my arm.

"The same people who murdered the metalworkers tried to murder me," I replied. Behind me, Robert growled. "Do you have any bandages?"

Mare wiped her hands, then she grabbed a small clay jar. "It's yarrow," she said, when Robert barred her from getting too close to me. "Sprinkle it on the wound to stop the bleeding. I'll get some clean linen."

Robert opened the jar and smelled it. "Aye, please fetch the linen," he said, as he crushed the dried flowers between his fingers and pressed it into the lacerations on my arm. "Fetch Rudrick, as well."

After Mare scurried off, Robert focused on my arm. "How bad is it?"

"It's not great, but I'll live." I glanced down. The bleeding had stopped, and the pain had lessened. "That yarrow seems to be helping." Robert paused with his hand on my shoulder. I covered it with my own. "I'm okay. Promise."

He nodded, then he kissed my forehead. "The one that struck you. You said you hurt them back?"

"Yeah, but if you want to beat her up a little more, I'm okay with it."

"Karina love, only you can make me smile at times like this."

"Times like what, now?" Rudrick said as he entered the kitchen. "Mare says you had a mishap, is that correct?"

"Yeah, it happened when the caits attacked us in the smithy," I replied. "How long have you been selling those fancy spears to the Unseelie?" When Rudrick blanched, and Robert only stared at me, I continued, "That's what's happening, isn't it? You've been selling weapons to the Unseelie, and I'm guessing the caits are the middlemen. The dwarves found out what you were doing, and refused to give you any more ore, because they know Fionnlagh doesn't like it when people break his rules."

"You dare to refer to our king by his name?" Rudrick asked.

"I dare a hell of a lot more than that," I said. "What happened to the metalworkers? Did you kill them so they'd keep your secrets?"

"We killed them," Nes said. Her hand was pressed against her side, and blood seeped between her fingers. I'd gotten her good. "Rudrick hired us to kill them all."

"Why did you lie to us earlier?" Robert demanded.

Nes shrugged. "We didn't know what you were up to, so we told you we were sent by Nicnevin. We are beholden to her, after all. And you don't quite have everything figured out. It was the metalworkers who first understood Rudrick's plans, and they refused to work. That was why he had them killed."

"And you went along with it," Robert said.

"Are you judging me on my kills, gallowglass?" Nes said. "How many lives have you ended, all because your mistress ordered it? We're killers. It's what we do."

"Robert is nothing like you," I began, then Robert put his hand on my shoulder.

"How did you escape the shadows?" he asked Nes.

"I was near the door, and the sunlight thinned them out," she replied.

"Next time, make them thicker," I said to Robert.

"You wielded the shadows, warrior?" Nes asked, then she laughed. "As if you're a living sluagh? Surely only a fool would play at being damned."

"Perhaps I am a living sluagh," Robert began. "And I've no doubt I'm damned." He raised his hand, and beckoned all the shadows in the kitchen into the palm of his hand. "But I am also the gallowglass, which makes me the Seelie's tool of vengeance. And right now, that vengeance is directed at you."

He flicked his hand, and shadows wrapped themselves around Nes like so many black veils. She opened her mouth to scream, and the darkness rushed down her throat.

In his wisest move yet, Rudrick backed toward the door. Robert spotted him, and threw his sgian dubh, a small dagger he kept in his belt. It missed Rudrick's body, but pierced his shirt near his left arm and pinned him against the doorframe.

"Move again, and I'll aim for your heart," Robert said.

"Nice throw," I said, as I watched Nes writhe on the floor. I liked to think I didn't hold grudges, but if she choked to death on the shadows, I wouldn't miss her. "What now?"

"Now, we call the king to deal with the criminals."

Fionnlagh responded to Robert's summons almost at once, and appeared in all his Seelie glory to mete out justice. Unfortunately, he brought Nicnevin with him.

"Good work, Robert," Fionnlagh said, as he surveyed the caits in the mass of darkness. We'd brought Rudrick outside, and tied him up next to the smithy. "The innkeeper was behind this scheme?"

"So it appears," Robert replied. "When the metalworkers learned who was purchasing the spears, and they refused to go along with his plans, the innkeeper hired the caits to murder them."

"The caits are rather efficient killers," Nicnevin said. "Almost as efficient as you, Robert."

I narrowed my eyes at her, and said to Fionnlagh, "All of the caits have been accounted for, but we don't know if anyone else in the village was complicit in Rudrick's plans. Would you like us to interview the villagers?"

"That won't be necessary," Fionnlagh said. "I'll punish Rudrick such a way to keep the rest from acting out."

"What about Mare?" I asked.

"The kitchen girl?" Fionnlagh countered. "What of her?"

"Yeah. She helped us, and she wasn't in with Rudrick. Shouldn't she get a reward?"

Fionnlagh glanced at Robert. "Is this true?"

"Aye," Robert replied. "Without Mare's help, we might not have discovered the innkeeper's true plans."

"Give her the inn," Nicnevin said. "All women need a way to make their own money. No one wants to solely rely on a man," she added, with a sly glance toward her husband.

"What a tragedy that would be," Fionnlagh said dryly. "As for Mare, she is absolved of any guilt. Should she like to run the inn, she may do so as she sees fit, but only after I've removed the Unseelie taint. After the land has been cleansed, the shadows should dissipate as well. Although, how a mere innkeeper managed to conscript caits and shades to his cause is a mystery to me."

"I trapped the caits in shadow," Robert said. Fionnlagh paused, and fixed Robert and me in his gaze. "A group of sluagh latched onto me in the moral realm. After a bit of back and forth, they agreed to follow me, and do my bidding."

Fionnlagh's brow pinched. "I must say, this is an unexpected, but useful, skill you have developed. Well done, Robert."

"So, you didn't send the sluagh to help him?" I asked. "Either of you?"

"I certainly didn't," Nicnevin said. "I like to be the only one in my shadows. But if you'd ever like assistance navigating the dark—"

"Nicnevin," Fionnlagh said. "Enough."

The Seelie Queen pouted. "Very well. Good luck with your shades, and your mortal lover. Only you could inspire such devotion among the dead and the living, Robert. Use your new talents well."

With that, the Seelie pair disappeared from view, along with the caits and Rudrick. What remained was the giant glob of shifting shadows.

"We should probably clean that up," I said. Robert raised his hand, and the shadows promptly coalesced into a ball in his palm. He watched the black orb for a moment, frowning.

"What is it?" I asked.

"They truly wanted to help me," Robert murmured. "I misjudged them."

"But once you knew better, you did better," I said. "That's the best anyone can do. And you did complete your mission."

"Aye, with help from you, and them," he said. "I suppose everything has worked out for the best."

"It sure has. What will you do with them?" I asked, nodding toward the shadows in his hand.

"I don't think I'll do anything," he replied. "I've spent enough time in the shadows. If the sluagh like it here in Elphame, then here they shall remain." Robert waved his other hand over the shadows, and they dispersed into the landscape. "From now on, Karina love, I shall live my life in the sunlight, with you."

I watched the shadows slide into the darkened crevices in and around the smithy. "That's your best plan yet."

Life in the Sunlight

After the king and his miserable wife left with the caits and innkeeper in tow, Karina and I advised Mare than the inn was now hers to do with as she wished, as soon as Fionnlagh deemed the land clean. She was pleased, and a bit apprehensive, since running such a place was no small task. She assured us she was up for it, and asked Karina and I if we'd like to stay on for a time.

"It's not that I didn't appreciate her offer," Karina said. We were back in our cottage in Crail, seated on the couch and watching that box of images she so enjoyed. "But we belong here."

I held out my arm, and Karina fit herself against my side. "Aye, love," I said, as I kissed her hair. "That we do. I much prefer these modern hot showers to bathing in a cold stream."

"That's what you like best about the mortal world? Indoor plumbing?"

I laughed, and held her a bit tighter. "I only prefer them because you join me in those showers."

Later on, I left Karina in the kitchen with her brother, where they discussed his latest writing. It was close to sunset, and I went out to the garden and watched the lengthening shadows. Soon enough, a few of the shadows approached me.

"I suppose I'm doomed to have you follow me for eternity?" I asked the sluagh.

"Not eternity," they replied as one. "You will die eventually."

I laughed through my nose. "You're right about that." I turned toward the cottage, and watched Karina as she sat at the table with her brother. She was smiling, and gesturing wildly, and so full of life and happiness I couldn't imagine her ever being comfortable with the sluagh nearby.

"I've given you your freedom," I said to the shades. "You needn't follow me."

"We remain honor bound to you," the shades replied, as they swirled around me. "We will depart, but should you need us, we will do your bidding."

The shades faded from view, which was for the best. I appreciated their devotion, but I did not want to get too comfortable wielding shadows and darkness. For too long, darkness had been my ally, but things were different now. I was different. From now on, I would face my challenges in the light, with Karina by my side. I may command the shades of Elphame, but I'll never be one of them.

If this is your first time meeting Karina and Robert, I hope you enjoyed reading about them as much as I enjoyed writing about this latest foray into Elphame. If you'd like to read more of their story, the titles are available wherever books are sold (or borrowed, in the case of libraries) or online as follows:

Gallowglass https://books2read.com/gallowglass
Walker https://books2read.com/walker-gallowglass2
Homecoming https://books2read.com/homecoming-gallowglass3

Also By Jennifer Allis Provost

The Chronicles of Parthalan, a six volume epic fantasy (and one short story collection)
Heir to the Sun
The Virgin Queen
Rise of the Deva'shi
Pieces of Parthalan: Six All-New Stories From The Land Of Parthalan
Golem
Elfsong
Sunfall

The Copper Legacy, a four book urban fantasy:
Copper Girl
Copper Ravens
Copper Veins
Copper Princess

A duology based in the Copper world:
Redemption
Salvation

Poison Garden, an urban fantasy filled with seers, witches, and one seriously hot detective:
Belladonna
Oleander
Bleeding Hearts
Thornapple
Wolfsbane
Mistletoe
Mandrake

Gallowglass, an urban fantasy set in Scotland and New York:
Gallowglass
Walker
Homecoming
Winter's Queen, an urban fantasy set in Scotland and Elphame:
Touch of Frost
Giant's Daughter
Elphame's Queen
Merrowkin, an urban fantasy set in Ireland above and below
Merrowkin
Death's Door
Manannán's Pearl
Changes, a contemporary romance:
Changing Teams
Changing Scenes
Changing Fate
Changing Dates

About The Author

Jennifer Allis Provost is a native New Englander who lives in a sprawling colonial along with her beautiful and precocious twins, a dog that thinks she's a kangaroo, a parrot, a junkyard cat, and a wonderful husband who never forgets to buy ice cream. As a child, she read anything and everything she could get her hands on, including a set of encyclopedias, but fantasy was always her favorite. She spends her days drinking vast amounts of coffee, arguing with her computer, and avoiding any and all domestic behavior.

Find Jenn on the web here: http://authorjenniferallisprovost.com/

For up to the minute sale notifications, follow her on Bookbub here: https://www.bookbub.com/profile/jennifer-allis-provost
    For exclusive content, follow her on Patreon: https://www.patreon.com/jenniferallisprovost/
    Friend her on Facebook: http://www.facebook.com/jennallis
    Follow her on Instagram: @jenniferaprovost
    Happy reading!

www.ingramcontent.com/pod-product-compliance
Lightning Source LLC
LaVergne TN
LVHW041713060526
838201LV00043B/708